THE CASE OF THE
DEAD MAN'S RING
BOOK ONE

Ryan Field

For more information contact:
Riverdale Avenue Books
5676 Riverdale Avenue
Riverdale, NY 10471
www.riverdaleavebooks.com

Design by www.formatting4U.com
Cover by Scott Carpenter

Digital ISBN 978-1-62601-726-9
Print ISBN 978-1-62601-727-6

Previously published in 2009, Ravenous Romance.
Second edition, Ryan Field Press, 2015

Riverdale Avenue Books would like to thank you for reading this copy of *The
Rainbow Detective Agency, Book 1: The Case of the Dead Man's Ring* by gifting
you one free book from each imprint, which you can download at the link provided:
https://preview.mailerlite.io/preview/1098983/sites/136486432257607665/0kJ9TD

If you are interested in being in our ARC reader/reviewer program, you can sign
up here. Reviews are the life blood of the independent author and publisher and
every single one counts to getting books into the hands of the right readers.

Dwayne Calvin

Dwayne Calvin's lover was still sleeping, facing the opposite direction, curled up under the covers on his side. Dwayne could only see the back of his head and his left shoulder. When Dwayne glanced at the chipped crystal clock on the nightstand and saw it was already a few minutes before 6:00 a.m., he leaned over gently and kissed his lover on the shoulder without waking him.

He climbed out of bed and went to the bathroom. It took him less than three minutes to put on the running gear he'd left hanging on a hook on the bathroom door.

In the kitchen, he grabbed his house key and a small case that contained his iPhone and personal identification. He took a gold ring from a dish above the kitchen sink and slipped it onto his ring finger. He never left the condo without the ring.

The park was only a block away from his condo building and he walked there at a brisk pace. Although he had a feeling the temperature would rise into the mid-80's today, it was only in the upper sixties this early in the morning. He tried to run faster to warm up but he was still sluggish from staying out late the night before.

When he finally broke into what felt like a decent stride, he veered off the main path and ran toward a heavily wooded section of the park. There was a small creek not far away and he enjoyed running along its rocky banks. Though the path alongside the creek was narrower and he had to pay attention to each step he took, it was one of the most peaceful private places he knew in a city as large and crowded as Los Angeles.

By the time Dwayne glanced at his watch and noticed he'd been running for a half hour, he figured he'd gone about three miles, and it was time to turn back. But as he slowed down so he could turn around and follow the same path back to his condo, he noticed a tall, dark guy walking barefoot in the woods, about 20 feet away. The guy wasn't wearing running gear; just baggy jeans that sagged on his hips and a black T-shirt that looked two sizes too large. For a second, Dwayne wondered why he was walking around that early in the morning in his bare feet. But he stopped wondering when he saw the guy had tattoos all over his arms and four or five different pierced sections on his face, including a thick bar through the bottom of his nose.

Dwayne figured he was one of those shy emo guys on his way to school. There was a small college on the other side of the park and the students usually cut through the park to get there. It was one of those community colleges where they taught humanities and trades at the same time. There was something experimental about it, Dwayne had read in the newspaper. Dwayne figured this guy looked as if he might be studying something that had more to do with construction than learning Shakespeare.

So Dwayne continued running back to where he'd started out, without giving the guy a second glance. But when he approached a narrow section where there was a fork, he heard leaves crunching behind him. He glanced back fast and saw the guy with the bare feet running right behind him. Instead of turning left and following the path back to the main section of the park, Dwayne decided to lose this guy in the bare feet and take a shortcut by veering to the right. He knew this would lead him father away from the entrance that was closest to his condo building. It would also lead him closer to another entrance that led to a main street where he would be safe.

But the barefoot guy turned right and followed him into a dark section lined with tall trees. Dwayne clenched his fists and took a quick breath. He figured if he sped up, he'd lose the idiot. Evidently, he was wrong. The guy with bare feet not only ran faster, but he also caught up with Dwayne and started running alongside him.

There weren't many options. With a surge of energy that came from somewhere deep down in his body, Dwayne made a quick turn and ran in the opposite direction to get away from him. He figured if he could get to the street, where there were people and cars, he could disappear. He never ran so fast or took such long strides in all the years he'd been running for pleasure. By the time he reached the end of the dark tunnel beneath the bridge, he glanced back and saw the young guy was still chasing him.

When Dwayne reached the clear, open section of the park, not far from the street, it was even more isolated than the other side of the park had been. Where the hell were all the people? Dwayne didn't stop. He clenched his fists and ran with the kind of speed runners only use when they are competing or running away from something dangerous. It was too intense to speak; he couldn't scream for help. He had to concentrate on the unfamiliar terrain so he wouldn't trip and fall. Sweat poured from his body, and his heart raced so fast he felt his chest pounding. When he finally saw the park entrance and heard traffic moving up and down the street, he felt such a wave of relief he smiled. But when he reached the street, he didn't stop to check the oncoming traffic and a huge black SUV smacked into him so fast he didn't even hear the driver blow the horn.

Before he closed his eyes, he was the only one who noticed the barefoot jogger had removed the gold ring from his finger.

Chapter One

After a long, hot soak in his garden tub, Proctor jumped into the shower and shaved his legs, armpits, and all visible pubic hair. It had been the worst morning of his life. His personal chef had taken a tantrum and quit, almost destroying the entire kitchen. His most recent lover had run out the back door in his underwear. Proctor's personal assistant, Jane, had informed him all the checks he'd been writing for the past few weeks had been bouncing. And now he was on his way to see his attorney to get some answers.

He styled his hair to make it look messy. He spritzed a fine, even coat of the best spray tan money could buy all over his body and dabbed it gently with a black towel. He didn't want too much spray tan; there was a fine line between too much, not enough, and just the right amount. He'd had special lighting installed in his white marble bathroom so he'd never make any mistakes with spray tan.

When he came out of the bathroom, he put on casual jeans that had cost him $1,600 at a boutique on Rodeo Drive in Beverly Hills. He'd only worn them once. Over the jeans, he wore a white Armani dress shirt and didn't tuck it in. His shoes were brown Gucci loafers, without socks. The only jewelry he ever wore was one of a dozen expensive watches. Today, he chose the Rolex.

When he went downstairs, he noticed the mess his high-strung chef had made was all cleaned up and Jane had lined his rock crystal collection up in neat little rows on a mirrored table in the center hall. It didn't look like any of the rock crystal was broken, not even the tall obelisk with malachite trim. They didn't look bad on the table either. Jane was his lifesaver, not just his personal assistant. He didn't know how he would be able to survive without Jane if she decided to quit. How she'd managed to clean up the mess and move the broken cabinet out of there so fast was anyone's guess. It would have taken Proctor the rest of the day just to pick up the rock crystal and line it up on the hall table.

He glanced down and smiled. His large spotted cat named Constance was sitting beneath the mirrored table, watching every move he made. For a Bengal cat, she wasn't as aggressive and lively as he'd hoped she would be. And she was only three years old. She tended to sleep too much, eat too much, and she couldn't have cared less about going outside. A bird could land on her head, and she wouldn't have flinched. She was timid, too. The slightest noise out of the ordinary sent her sailing under a table or into a corner. His friends said he was lucky she was so calm and serene; they said he shouldn't complain. Some Bengal cats could be rambunctious. But he wanted a domestic cat with the personality of a wildcat, not a big old lazy hound dog that was afraid of her shadow. Once in a while, if Constance disliked someone intensely, she would hiss and growl at them. But that didn't happen often.

He bent down and patted the top of her head, and she purred. "Don't worry, sweetie. You're no lion, but I love ya just as much. Where's Jane? I don't see her anywhere." He often talked to Constance as if she understood every word he said. Sometimes, if she glanced at him in the right way, he thought she really did.

As he said this, Constance looked up and Jane said, "I've been out back getting rid of the cabinet. I took it apart and I'll put it out on trash day. I phoned your attorney, and you have an appointment in an hour."

"An hour?" That didn't give him much time to get into town and stop by his business manager's office. He'd been expecting to have at least two hours. "I made the appointment two hours ago," Jane said. She sent him a sarcastic look and frowned. "I didn't know it would take you that long to get ready."

Proctor smiled and crossed to the hall closet. He was used to her sarcasm by now. He pulled out a Louis Vuitton men's satchel and reached inside for his car keys.

Before he had a chance to ask about the car, Jane said, "I brought the Mercedes around. It's out front."

Proctor smiled and walked to where she was standing. He hugged her and said, "I don't know what I'd do without you. Please promise me you'll never leave."

Jane lifted an eyebrow and shrugged. "I'd just like to get paid."

Proctor waved his arm and turned to the door. "I'll straighten it all out this afternoon. I'm sure there's nothing to worry about."

* * *

He stopped by his business manager's office first, only the doors were locked, the office was empty, and the woman in the office next door said they'd moved out in the middle of the night earlier that month. When he reached his lawyer's building, the secretary escorted him right into the office without asking any questions. The secretary barely said two words and she wouldn't look him in the eye. His lawyer stood up from his desk and crossed the room to greet him.

The lawyer shook his hand, frowned, and said, "Please have a seat. I think you should be sitting down."

Proctor gulped. "I'd rather stand, Michael." Michael was a slender man in his early 60s. He was openly gay and he flirted with Proctor every time he saw him. He even had a framed, signed famous wet underwear poster of Proctor over his desk. But today he was frowning and speaking in a low, serious tone. He'd been Proctor's attorney for almost 10 years. Proctor had never seen him this somber in all that time, not even when they'd written up Proctor's last will and testament.

Michael reached for his hand and held it. "Are you sure?"

"Yes. I'm sure. I just came from my business manager's office and there's no one there. The entire office is empty and the woman next door said they've disappeared and no one knows where they went."

"That's why I've been trying to contact you."

"I've been very busy. You know I don't know anything about these things."

"They've taken almost everything you have."

Proctor gulped again. Last he'd heard, he was worth millions. "Huh?"

"They've embezzled almost everything and they've disappeared. There is a warrant out for their arrest, but I have a feeling they are long out of the country by now."

Proctor reached for the back of a chair. He felt lightheaded again, as if he might faint. "You've got to be joking. These things only happen on TV or in the movies. They don't happen in real life."

Michael frowned and sent him a look. "I wish I *were* joking."

"So that's why all my checks have been bouncing," Proctor said.

The attorney nodded.

"What the fuck am I going to do now? We have to find them and get my money back." His first thought was how good it would feel to have his hands around his business manager's neck.

"It's not that simple. They were taking small amounts over a long period of time and you never noticed. Evidently, from what I've seen, this has been going on for a long time."

"But I trusted them completely," Proctor said. "What kind of people would do such a thing?"

The attorney shrugged. "Bad people."

Proctor turned and walked toward the window. He clenched his fists and focused hard on his breathing so he wouldn't hyperventilate. His next thought was to hunt down the business manager and annihilate him with his bare hands and a baseball bat.

"They didn't get everything, though," Michael said.

Proctor turned around fast. "What do you mean? I still have money left?"

"You have a few non-liquid assets left," he said. He lifted a file from his desk and read, "There's a small gym over on Santa Monica Boulevard you own, a few stocks in some technology companies, five or six small businesses, and a private detective agency in Beverly Hills."

Proctor took a deep breath. He exhaled and said, "Okay, this sounds a little better. How much money do these things make?"

Michael read a few more things in silence and frowned. "More than a million dollars."

Proctor's head went up. "I made more than a million dollars with these businesses? That sounds promising. At least I can survive."

The lawyer frowned. "I'm afraid they don't make any money at all. They lost over $2,000,000. It seems your business manager bought these companies as write-offs."

Proctor's heart started beating faster. His face grew warm again. He felt like he'd been punched in the stomach twice in the same day. "I don't understand. What's the bottom line?"

"You're flat broke. You have nothing left."

* * *

On the way out to the parking lot, Michael guided Proctor to his car and offered consolation and advice. He understood the devastation and he offered positive suggestions about how to handle the situation. "You're going to be fine. You're Proctor Gamble. You made millions of dollars once. You'll do it again."

7

Proctor sighed and said, "I'm not in my 20s anymore. I'm 35 and I'm not exactly the hot commodity I once was." He never fooled himself into believing things that weren't true. It was a youth-oriented culture for everyone, and even more so when it came to men within the gay community.

"You'll be fine," Michael said. "There are all kinds of things you can do. I hear there's huge market for book cover models. Five years ago, you were the most sought after male model in the world. A lot of publishers would love to get you now."

"Oh, dear God," Proctor said. "I never thought my headless torso might wind up on the cover of a BDSM book with a title like *The Agony and Ecstasy of It All*." It seemed to just get worse and worse the more he thought about his options.

"There are trade shows and magazines for men of advanced ages. I'm sure there are plenty of things you can do."

Proctor lifted his hand and said, "Please stop. I don't need to hear this right now. I'm already depressed enough." The sad fact was Proctor hadn't had any decent offers to model in a long time. The jobs started slowing down after he turned 30, and they continued to do so. Ten years earlier, he'd been able to pick and choose his offers with the kind of arrogance most people never experience for one day in their lives.

Michael opened the car door for him and reached for his shoulder. "I'm going to advance you some money until you get things straightened out. In the meantime, here's a list of all the businesses you own. I want you to get on this right away. Go to each one and ask if they are willing to buy you out. Most probably will. If they won't, you're going to have to close them down. You can't afford any more losses: debt is the last thing you need now."

Proctor nodded slowly and sat down in the car. On top of all this, now he had to be responsible for other people losing their jobs. He felt a sting in his eye and held back so he wouldn't cry in front of Michael. He looked up and said, "This is the worst thing that's ever happened to me. I can't be poor. I'd rather be ugly than poor. I'd rather be fat than poor. I'd rather have a little dick and a bald head than be poor. *I don't know how to be poor*."

Michael bent down and kissed him on the cheek. "You're going to be okay. You still have the hottest ass and face in town. Get out there and make it work for you like you've always done."

Chapter Two

By the end of the following week, Proctor had either sold his portions of the small businesses to the other owners, or he'd given them notice and shut them down. Most were willing to buy him out, and he managed to get enough cash to pay the loan back to his lawyer and have enough on which to get by for the next six months. The ones he had to shut down didn't seem to mind much; they'd been expecting it. Jane agreed to stay on as his personal assistant for less pay and free room and board. But there wouldn't be a chef, maid, or driver anymore, and Proctor would have to learn how to care for his own property and clean his own swimming pool for a while.

The only business he couldn't shut down was a small pet shop/pet grooming parlor in West Hollywood. The owner was such a nice older gay man, with a plump, jolly build and fuzzy white eyebrows Proctor didn't have the heart. His name was Noah, and the shop was called Noah's Little Ark. The kittens and puppies in the shop tugged at Proctor's heart. Chubby Noah almost cried when he said he couldn't afford to buy Proctor out. He lived on a fixed income and worked the shop all by himself seven days a week. There was no way Proctor would be responsible for ruining the life of such a nice, harmless little man who depended on the small income this pet shop generated. There was no way he would be responsible for something bad happening to all those adorable little puppies and kittens. So, Proctor gave the old guy a hug and said he'd keep in touch. He told him the shop looked wonderful with the blue and white gingham curtains and the hideous bright yellow walls. Then Proctor went back home and phoned his agent and told him to find modeling work as fast as he could. He made it clear he wasn't above doing anything to make money. He'd even consider posing in the nude if that was what it took, which was something he'd never done before.

The very last business investment Proctor visited turned out to be

9

interesting. This was the private investigation firm called Exotique Private Investigation Agency. The other businesses were all rinky dink start-ups, and this one seemed higher tech and professional, at first glance. The suite of offices was located in a posh section of Beverly Hills, in a building that had been designed by a well-known Los Angeles architect. Proctor's dentist was there and he knew the building fairly well.

When Proctor parked in a private gated parking lot next to the building, he climbed out of the car, glanced up, and pressed his lips together. According to what he'd read in Michael's papers, this was the business that lost the least amount of money but also cost the most to keep running. It was also named after the underwear company that had helped make Proctor Gamble a famous household name, Exotique. Proctor wasn't sure whether this was a good sign or not. It worked for underwear. But it sounded a little too contrived for the name of a serious private investigation firm.

When he stepped off the elevator on the third floor and walked to the suite, the door swung open and a tall, gorgeous blond man walked out into the hallway. The blond guy wore a tight athletic suit and carried one of those portable massage tables in one hand and a wad of cash in the other. He smiled at Proctor, looked him up and down, and continued walking to the elevator. When Proctor glanced back, the blond guy smiled and winked. Proctor wondered what on earth someone like that would be doing in a private investigation agency.

The dowdy young man at the main reception desk looked up when Proctor entered the office. He winked at Proctor and reached to pick up the telephone. He said, "Exotique Private Investigation Agency. You lost it, we'll find it. You need it, we'll get it. There's nothing we can't handle, we could find it with a candle. We also take all credit cards, cash, and personal checks. What can I do for you on this bright, wonderful day?"

Proctor pressed his palm to his throat. This was beginning to feel like a bad dream.

There was a moment of silence, then the young man frowned and said, "I'm sorry. You're looking for the Chinese takeout down the street. A lot of people get us confused."

When he hung up, he set the receiver down and sighed. The poor thing reminded Proctor of a kid he'd gone to high school with. He had thick, unruly, black curly hair, heavy dark eyeglasses that sloped down on the bridge of his nose, and a weak chin that sank into his neck. He was wearing a yellow and white checked short sleeved shirt and a clip-on brown tie. He looked more like he worked in a convenience store than an upscale detective agency. All that was missing was a name tag. He gazed at Proctor as if he were seeing a mirage, and said, "You're gorgeous. What can I do for you?"

He seemed like a nice enough guy, and he was obviously gay. But proctor didn't want to waste time. He didn't want to get to know anyone here. From what he could see, there were other employees walking around and sitting at desks, and no one looked like they were actually doing any work. "I'd like to speak with whoever is in charge," Proctor said.

When he thought about all the money he was spending keeping this place going, at a loss, he clenched his fists and took a quick breath. He had to be strong. He had to do this, no matter how hard it was.

The young man stood up and said, "I'm Alvin Schlock. If you'll follow me, I'll take you back to Mr. Huntingdon's office. He should be dressed by now."

"*Dressed*?"

"He just had a visit from his personal masseur."

"Oh, brother." On company time and paid with the company expense account, no doubt.

Alvin led Proctor through a short corridor to a rear office. Unlike all the other businesses Proctor owned, this one was in a building with exquisite art, new carpets, and freshly painted walls in neutral shades. It didn't look as if there were any expenses being spared. Poor Alvin walked like a duck, with his feet splayed and his knees knocking together. He didn't seem to fit into the setting very well. He would have fit in better at the pet shop in West Hollywood with the chubby older man and the tacky gingham curtains. When they reached a door with a sign that read, "Blair Huntingdon, President," Alvin knocked a few times and opened the door without waiting for a response.

A basketball flew through the room. It hit Alvin in the face and knocked his heavy eyeglasses sideways.

Proctor glanced at Alvin and blinked. This was getting bizarre. Then he looked across the room at a tall handsome man with short dark hair and said, "Hello. I see you're dressed."

"Well," said the man. Then he pursed his lips and glanced down at Proctor's crotch. "I can take my clothes off if that would make you happy."

"Don't flatter yourself," Proctor said.

Blair Huntingdon made an attempt to bow, as if to royalty, and said, "As you wish, Your Royal Highness."

Proctor sent him a glare. He assumed this was Blair Huntingdon, so-called president of the agency, the agency that was losing Proctor money every year. He was younger and better looking than Proctor would have imagined a private detective would be. Proctor had pictured a seedy, unkempt guy, with a wrinkled suit, a bad haircut, and cheap shoes, like he'd seen on old TV shows. But Blair wore a crisp white dress shirt, an expensive tie, and perfectly pressed slacks that looked as if they were part of a deep navy Versace suit. Proctor would have bet money his black shoes were Prada, and he didn't have much to bet. So this was where all his hard-earned money was going. He was keeping an aging rent boy in designer clothes and massages, so he could shoot hoops in an office that cost more money to maintain than Proctor wanted to think about.

Blair crossed the room and reached for the basketball in Alvin's arms. He grabbed it fast and tossed it over his shoulder without looking. It landed in the middle of an empty wastebasket, as if he'd been practicing this move for way too long. "You're looking good today, Alvin." He patted Alvin on the back. "Yellow is definitely your color. Not everyone can wear yellow. Not everyone *would* wear yellow. But with your thick hair, you make it work, baby."

Proctor rolled his eyes. The guy was full of shit.

Blair glanced at Proctor, and asked Alvin, "Who is *this* fine man with such high cheekbones and smooth skin?"

Proctor didn't say a word; he wasn't impressed. He knew a fast-talking con man the minute he saw one. This one, indeed, happened to be better looking than most. He had a way about him that seemed nicer than most. But Proctor wasn't about to let anyone change his mind about closing this place down.

Alvin tried to speak, but Blair wouldn't let him. Blair placed his hand on Alvin's back, turned him around, and said, "You go back out front and look pretty, Alvin. Don't forget to smile and show those sexy dimples." Then he shoved him into the hall, closed the door, and guided Proctor to his desk with his hand on the small of Proctor's back.

Proctor went along without resistance. Even though he hadn't expected it, he knew Blair was gay, and Blair was slick and intense enough to know he was gay. Neither of them needed to pretend with each other. It didn't always happen this way. Some gay men were harder to read than others. But once in a while, when Proctor met a man with whom he felt an unusual connection, he didn't have to question the man's sexuality.

The flirting and cajoling continued on Blair's end. He was obviously the dominant type. Blair led him to the desk, and then he sat down on the desktop and faced him. He smiled and talked so fast about absolutely nothing significant, Proctor had trouble keeping up with him. Blair gazed at Proctor's lips and took quick looks at Proctor's crotch between sentences. He seemed to be talking about the way he'd saved poor Alvin's life. He said he'd practically found Alvin on the street after he'd been kicked out of his family home for being gay. Blair had given him a job at the agency, taught him the basics of gay life, and filled him with self confidence so he'd be a man. For a moment, it sounded as if Blair alone had been responsible for everything and anything poor little Alvin did.

At one point, while Blair rambled on about how much weight Alvin had lost since he'd first started working there, Proctor sent Blair a deadpan stare and said, "And all this concerns me in what way?"

This time Blair blinked. "I'm sorry. What you just said doesn't *parse* well."

"Give me a break, man," Proctor said. "It *parsed* all right. And who the hell uses words like *parse*, anyway? I can't believe I'm actually having this conversation." He leaned forward without blinking and said, "I'm not interested in Alvin."

Without missing a beat, Blair said, "I didn't think you were. But don't worry. We're going to take good care of you here at Exotique. Your worries are over. We'll get to the bottom of whatever your problem is. No matter how sleazy or nasty it is, we'll take care of you." Then he spread his legs wider, glanced sideways at Proctor's ass, and licked his lips. "I'll bet you've been a very naughty boy with someone's husband, haven't you? I can't imagine that *your* husband would be cheating on you. You're way too hot."

Proctor smiled. Though he was frustrated, he hadn't been this amused in a long time. "Cut the bullshit." He remained calm and relaxed. "We need to get down to business."

Blair slid off the desk. He didn't seem insulted or upset. "Okay, no more bullshit. I like honesty. I can see you're serious and you want to get down to business." He extended his right hand and said, "I'm Blair Huntingdon and you're…"

"Proctor Gamble."

He spoke over Proctor. "Proctor Gamble. You look very familiar to me. I'm sure we've met. I know the name from somewhere." He glanced at Proctor's ass again. "I know the face, too."

"Nope," Proctor said. He sighed and forced back the urge to yawn. "I can assure you we've never crossed paths. I'd never forget *you*, trust me."

Blair's tone became somber. He put on his suit jacket, as if trying to appear more professional, and turned to face Proctor. "Oh no, I never forget an incredible face or an ass. And you have both."

Proctor rolled his eyes, wondering if Blair ever stopped yammering.

"I'll get it," Blair said. "Just give me a minute. My mind is a steel trap. Once I get something in there, it's there forever."

"Seriously," Proctor said. "We've never met. Take my word for it." This time he wanted to smile wider. He couldn't resist this guy's charming tenacity. There was something both adorable and dangerous about him. But Proctor held back the smile, because he didn't want Blair to think he was softening. Getting friendly with this guy wouldn't make what he had to do any easier.

"It'll come to me," Blair said. He tapped his chin with his index finger and tried to look serious. It didn't work.

"Can't we just get down to business?" Proctor said. "I don't have time to waste."

"Give me a hint. Give me something to work with. I know I've seen you before."

Proctor inhaled and let out a deep breath. "Okay. Maybe you've seen photos of me. There was one that was very well known." He hated to brag about his past, especially the underwear photo that had made him famous.

When Proctor said this, Blair smacked his palms together and said, "That's it. I knew it. I could tell by the way you look in those tight jeans. I'd recognize that ass anywhere."

"I *beg* your pardon." His ass had nothing to do with it. The famous photo had been frontal, not rear.

"Oh, don't be shy with me," Blair said. "You know you've got a great ass. Why pretend it doesn't exist? I'm an ass man myself. I always have been. I never forget a great one, either."

"Thank you," Proctor said. "I'm sure you have a nice ass, too. Now can we get down to the reason why I'm here?"

"I'm thinking around the year 2000," Blair said. He spoke fast again.

14

"I'd bet my life you were the January centerfold in *Inches*. Back then, when magazines were more popular, I never missed an issue. Not that I'm a porn freak or anything, but I do check it out sometimes when I'm bored. From what I recall, you measured in with about nine inches, cut. You were that little hottie who loved to read for entertainment, your favorite movie was *Moonstruck*, and your favorite entertainer was Cher. You were also versatile and preferred men without facial hair. I kind of pictured you to be the more effeminate, prissy type. But hell, you're almost as butch as I am."

Proctor squared his shoulders and clenched his fists. He hated it when dominant, aggressive men like Blair formed opinions about him without knowing facts. "I can promise you that I've never been in a magazine called *Inches*. I've never posed *nude* anywhere in my life as a centerfold model. I don't own anything ever recorded by Cher and I've never seen *Moonstruck*. And I couldn't care less what you think of me." He *was* almost nine inches cut, but he decided this was none of Blair's business.

Only Blair didn't seem to be paying attention to him. He said, "After that, you did a few movies under the stage name Dude Buckster. One movie in particular was titled *Power Bottom Boi*, and you were the star. From what I remember, you were one hell of a power bottom, too. You must have taken on 40 or 50 guys in the one scene where you were over a barrel, legs wide open for the boys."

Proctor's head jerked to the side. "I'll have you know I've never done porn, nor have I ever been over a barrel with 50 men behind me. I've never used a stage name. Proctor Gamble is my *real* name. My father had a sense of humor I'm still trying to get over. My father wanted to name my sister Proctor Ann Gamble, but my mother refused to give in that time, and they just called her Ann. So he settled on Proctor with me."

Blair shrugged. "It serves you well. Proctor is a great name. It's like Armie Hammer. Get it? *Arm & Hammer*? You never forget it once you hear it."

People were always getting Proctor mixed up with Armie Hammer. This made his skin crawl. Mostly because they didn't get Armie Hammer mixed up with Proctor.

"I hope you don't mind my honesty," Blair said. "But you are even hotter now than you were back then. I've never seen a guy get so much better with time. You are absolutely flawless. And that ass goes without saying."

Though Proctor knew false flattery when he heard it, his face softened and he almost smiled. Blair's voice came off so smooth and sincere, it was hard to resist his charm. Proctor figured he was either the same age or a few years younger.

"I can't believe I'm standing across from the best power bottom of all time right now, fully dressed, with both feet on the floor." He walked to where Proctor stood, looked into his eyes, and said, "Damn," with an exasperated stage whisper. Then he reached around, without asking for permission, and set his hand on Proctor's ass. "I'm all top myself, just in case you have an itch that might need to be scratched."

Proctor had had enough. He grabbed Blair's hand and yanked it off his ass. He stepped away, squared his back, and said, "Let's get one thing clear, buddy." He lowered his tone and leaned forward. "I'm not this so-called power bottom you're talking about. I've never posed for *Inches* or any other pornster magazine. I've never done a porn film and I've never been paid to have sex with anyone. Just so it's clear, and listen to me closely, so I don't have to repeat myself again, I'm Mr. Proctor Gamble and I own you and this half-assed business you call a detective agency."

The part about Proctor owning the agency seemed to fly right over Blair's head. He looked down and thought for a moment. When he lifted his head he said, "Proctor Gamble. That's it. Proctor Gamble. You're the Proctor Gamble of the Exotique Underwear photo from 10 years ago. That's you? Are you telling me that's who is standing here in front of me now?" He pointed at Proctor, as if he couldn't get over the shock. "Exotique men's underwear, the only underwear that's even better wet than it is dry." He smiled. He sent Proctor a look. "I still have that famous picture in my closet at home. I can't tell you how many wonderful nights I've experienced staring at it."

Proctor rolled his eyes. He'd learned to get over the fact that so many strange men used his image to jack off. "Okay, so I'm not a saint. But I never posed in the nude, either. There's a difference. I was wearing underwear that got wet by accident, and at the time I never thought it would become so popular. It was luck."

Blair smiled and looked at Proctor's ass. "Oh, baby, that was more than just luck. That ass and those legs were meant to be in wet panties."

"You're a real charmer," Proctor said. "I can't wait until you really start to compliment me."

"What? I'm honest. I see a great ass and I'm not ashamed to say so.

You can't fault a guy for knowing what he likes." He crossed to his chair and sat down behind the desk. "I have to tell you that I've always loved you. You're the hottest guy on the planet. Seriously. What can I do for you today? Anything you want."

When he asked this question, Proctor popped a Tic Tac into his mouth and said, "Clear out your desk. You're out of a job, buddy."

Blair continued to smile, as if he hadn't heard this. "I was thinking of framing your poster. Did I tell you how hot you are?"

Proctor reached into his satchel and pulled out a stack of papers. "Yes, you told me," he said. Then he proceeded to paraphrase the details to Blair, glancing down at the papers he'd read about 100 times the night before as practice. "Exotique Private Detective Agency is owned by Proctor Gamble Enterprises. You've been performing at a loss for a long time and due to personal financial setbacks I'm now forced to shut you down and recuperate my losses. This means all company credit cards, expense accounts, and all property belonging to this enterprise. Everything should be surrendered to me or my attorney, and please hand in the keys to all company cars immediately."

When he was finished with the basic details, Proctor shoved the papers back into his satchel and turned to leave the office. "A formal letter has already been sent to you."

For the first time since Proctor entered, Blair stopped smiling. He stood up and followed Proctor to the door. "You can't take my BMW. That's my *car*."

Proctor continued walking. "That's a company car." He didn't even turn around to look him in the eye. He had to be strong about this. He couldn't let a smooth talking, hot guy like Blair sweet talk him out of doing this.

When they were in the reception area, Blair said, "Wait. You can't just do this to me." He gestured to the rest of the open office. "And not to all these other people. These people are decent and hardworking. You can't just put them out on the street."

Proctor pushed the door open and stepped into the hall. Though his heart raced, he forced his tone to remain strong. "I would advise you to let your employees know what's happening as quickly as possible. Real estate agents have been notified and the office will be sublet as soon as possible. I hope you're paying attention to me because I'm not going to repeat myself. This is going to happen fast and there's nothing you can

17

do to stop it." His legs started to feel wobbly, and his mouth went dry. He walked faster; he wanted to get out of there as quickly as he could and forget this had ever happened. Most of all, he wanted to find his shifty business manager and hit him over the head with a hammer. "And, just so you know, I'm not used to being the cause of people losing their jobs. I wouldn't be doing this if it wasn't absolutely necessary."

Blair followed him right up to the elevator. When Proctor pushed the elevator button, Blair said, "I can't believe all these years I stared at that wet underwear photo I really thought you were someone special. I've seen you in magazine ads, on posters, and I even saw you do talk shows. For a while, I used to think you'd be a great spokesperson for the entire gay community. Damn, was I wrong. You couldn't care less. You're nothing more than another aging gay *cunt*."

At the exact moment Blair called him a cunt, the elevator doors opened, and Proctor turned to face him. If there was one word Proctor despised, it was that one. He never used it and he never tolerated anyone else using it. Without thinking, his arm went up, he made a fist, and he attempted to punch Blair in the face.

But Blair grabbed his wrist, held it tightly, and smiled. Then he pushed him into the elevator and pinned him to the wall. While the doors closed and the elevator went up to the next floor, Blair leaned forward and shoved his tongue into Proctor's mouth. At the same time, he unfastened Proctor's jeans and slid his hands into his pants.

While Blair made this bold move, Proctor tried to fight back. He pushed him, tried to turn his head, and shoved his knee between Blair's legs. But it all happened so fast there wasn't time to think clearly. When Proctor's jeans were down to his knees and Blair began to squeeze his ass and kiss him at the same time, he submitted and sank into Blair's arms. He grabbed the back of Blair's head and kissed him harder. When his jeans were down around his ankles and his white shirt was up over his shoulders, Blair reached back to stop the elevator before it reached the next floor.

The entire act took less than five minutes. When the elevator stopped between floors, Blair turned him around and slapped his ass. While Proctor braced his palms against the elevator wall and spread his legs, Blair pulled his dick out of his suit pants and put on a pre-lubed condom. Blair entered fast, with one quick plunge that made Proctor bite his fist and wince. Then Blair pulled Proctor back against his torso and started fucking so fast the entire world seemed to vibrate.

They both broke into a sweat. The only sounds were heavy breathing and Blair's pelvis smacking into Proctor's ass. At one point, Blair grabbed Proctor's head and turned it sideways so he could kiss him. Proctor reached down and grabbed his own dick. A minute after that, they both came at the same time, with their jaws locked together in what Proctor would one day describe as the most intense climax he'd ever had and probably ever would have. It was as if a million pent up emotions were released in one flash flood that lasted less than five minutes.

When it was over, Blair put his dick back into his pants without removing the condom. Proctor pulled down his shirt and pulled up his jeans. He took a deep breath and glanced down at the mess he'd made all over the elevator wall. He wished he had something to clean it up with. He hoped there was no one waiting to get into the elevator when it stopped in the lobby. His heart stopped when he looked up and saw a camera. "Oh shit. We're busted. This was all on video and security is probably laughing their asses off right now. And the last thing I need right now is something like this on the Internet."

"Don't sweat it," Blair said, smoothing out his pants. "I know those guys in security. I've done favors for all of them. I'll take care of it and no one will ever know."

Proctor fastened a button on his shirt so no one would suspect they'd just been fucking. "That's good to know."

A second before the elevator came to a halt in the lobby, Blair adjusted his suit jacket and he flung Proctor a huge smile. "I knew I was right about you. I'm always right in these cases."

Proctor had never done anything like this in a public place before. He felt as if everyone in the building knew what he'd just done in the elevator with a virtual stranger.

"What were you right about?" He thought Blair was going to say something warm and tender, like that he was right about Proctor not being so bad after all that he wasn't the c-word.

But Blair smiled even wider and said, "I knew you were a great power bottom. I could tell by the way you walked. That ass is solid gold, baby."

Proctor felt his face getting red again. He'd never been so insulted by a man in his life, especially not after sex. Usually they treated him like a prince. They always thanked him. When he turned and lifted his arm, this time he didn't miss. Blair didn't try to stop him, either. As the elevator stopped and the doors opened, Proctor punched him in the face, and he went down on his ass.

Blair shrugged. He sat up, rubbed his jaw, and smiled. He took the punch well. "I knew that was coming."

There was an older man waiting to get into the elevator. He stood there and gaped at them both.

Without looking back, Proctor left Blair on the floor and walked toward the main entrance. On the way out, he said, "You have to be the most insulting man I've ever met."

For a moment, he wondered if Blair would follow him out into the main lobby. But all he heard was Blair's voice call out from the elevator. "And you can't get enough of it. Have a good night, boss."

Chapter Three

When Proctor returned home, he plopped down on a long black leather bench in the front hall and kicked off his shoes. Constance crept over slowly and rubbed her spotted coat against his leg. Closing down businesses and firing people made his stomach pull in a way he'd never experienced before. A sharp tug that wouldn't go away and a constant feeling of being on the brink of nausea made him want to lean over and rock back and forth in despair.

He wished he hadn't punched Blair Huntingdon in the face. The poor guy had just lost his job, his car, and his entire way of life. Proctor knew how that felt; he knew the panic and fear Blair had to be experiencing. It was no wonder Blair called him a cunt. Proctor only wished he could find his sleazy business manager and call him a cunt one day soon.

All he wanted to do was go up to his room, rip off his clothes, and fall into bed. The backs of his legs were a little sore from the pounding he'd taken from Blair in the elevator. This was another reason he felt sorry about slapping Blair. The guy was pushy, rude, obnoxious, and presumptuous. Aside from all that, Proctor had never experienced such an exhilarating fuck in his life. If it hadn't been for all that unpleasant firing business, Proctor probably would have been energized.

When the phone rang, he picked up his shoes and stood. Jane could get the phone; she could take care of his phone calls until he felt more like himself. But as he started toward the stairs, Jane crossed into the hall and said, "It's Michael. He says it's important."

Proctor could see she had her hand over the mouthpiece. "Can't you just take a message? I'm exhausted. I ruined lives today. I've devastated people. I punched a man in the face. I need sleep." The deep tug in the middle of his stomach pulled again. "I'm going to wind up with an ulcer."

Jane shrugged. "He says you'll want to talk to him." She held out the phone.

Proctor dropped his shoes on the bench and took the phone. He squinted for a moment, then said, "Hi, Michael. What can I do for you?" He was hoping this had nothing to do with legal business. He had an appointment with Michael next week to go over all the businesses he'd liquidated.

"I have this friend," Michael said. "He's dying to go out with you. We were playing golf the other day and I mentioned you were a close friend. He says he's always been a huge fan and he's dying to meet you."

"Ah well. A blind date." He hadn't been on one of those in years.

"He recently broke up with his partner," Michael said. "And he's one of the most successful dentists in southern California. Who knows? You might hit it off."

"What does he look like?" Proctor asked.

"He's in his mid-50s, has a slim build, and he drives a Bentley."

This wasn't exactly the best description Michael could have given. But Proctor understood where Michael was going with this. Michael thought like a lawyer, with dollar signs crossing before his eyes, not like a human being. "What did you tell him?"

"I just said I'd let you know he's interested in going out with you and I'd give you his number. I said I didn't feel comfortable giving out your private number."

Proctor sighed. "Is he really a nice guy? There's nothing creepy or weird about him? Seriously, tell me the truth, Michael. Is he like into feet, or wearing lace panties? Will I have to spank him with a feather?"

"I play *golf* with him," Michael said. "I don't know how big his *dick* is. But I do know he seems basically decent. And he owns homes in Beverly Hills, Palm Springs, South Beach in Miami, and East Hampton, New York. All you have to do is go out with him once. If it doesn't work, you had a free meal in a nice place with a nice guy."

"How important is this to *you*?" Proctor knew Michael well by now. Like all the attorneys he'd ever known, there was always a hidden agenda. Even though Michael was insinuating Proctor might be able to snag a rich husband in the nick of time, he probably had his own ulterior motives for asking Proctor to go out with this guy.

"He's my best client," Michael said. "I handle all his legal affairs. He generates a lot of money for the firm."

"I see. What's his name?"

"Kent Russell," Michael said. Then he gave Proctor Kent's phone

22

number and told him to call as soon as he hung up. He said Kent would be waiting for his call.

* * *

While Proctor was on the phone with Kent Russell setting up his date that night, the young barefoot jogger with the pierced nose who had chased Dwayne through the park and into oncoming traffic was making his own phone call from a dark, seedy east Los Angeles hotel room that smelled like wet socks and moldy jock straps. Only he was naked now, and there was another young man with jet black hair sprawled out naked on his soiled sheets. The barefoot jogger had just fucked the slim young guy on the lumpy bed and left him drenched in sweat, face down, with his soft white legs wide open. They'd met in a public restroom that afternoon and the barefoot jogger had invited him back to his room.

This phone call couldn't wait. Even though the barefoot jogger wanted to go back to bed and rub his dick up and down the guy's sweet white ass, he had to get this business straightened out. He didn't want the guy in his bed to overhear the conversation, so he looped to the other side of the hotel room and stood naked in front of an open window that looked down on a back alley filled with trash cans and discarded debris. He smiled as a rat the size of a small dog jumped into a trash can. As he dialed, he noticed an older man in the building across the alley. The older man stood in the window slumped forward, groping his crotch, leering at the barefoot jogger's naked body, licking his lips. The barefoot jogger wasn't intimidated, and he didn't pull down the shade like most guys would have done. He turned so the old man would have a clear view of his body, grabbed his big floppy dick, and jerked it around with his left hand. He knew the old guys loved his type: tattooed everywhere, pierced facial features, and sleazy.

The old man's eyes widened. He pulled a small dick out of his boxer shorts and started groping with his thumb and index finger. The barefoot jogger dialed the phone number and waited for someone to pick up, leaning back and massaging his balls with his other hand. He figured it wouldn't hurt to give an old pervert queer a free show. It would be his good deed for the day. He probably had the best dick the old troll had seen in years.

A woman with a weak, gentle voice answered the phone and the barefoot jogger asked to speak with a man named Morris. The woman told him to hold on and she'd get him. While she was gone, the jogger overheard children laughing and people talking louder than usual. It sounded as if someone was shouting for someone else to blow out candles on a birthday cake. He knew Morris had a large family. He figured they were celebrating a kid's birthday.

A minute later, a deep throaty voice said, "Hello, this is Morris." He spoke with a German accent.

The barefoot jogger didn't say his name. He just said, "I've got it." He didn't say what he had, or go into any details. "And I need to get rid of it fast."

"I'll get it tomorrow night," Morris said. "I'm busy right now. I don't want to change the plan. No one is following you. You're fine."

The barefoot jogger turned sideways and started jerking his dick very slowly for the old man on the other side of the alley. He liked being naked in front of people; he didn't care what they looked like. It gave him a thrill that couldn't compare to anything else. "I'm not fine. I need to get rid of this now. Meet me tonight."

Morris sighed. "Okay. Meet me in an hour at the top floor restaurant I told you about in the hotel. No one would ever expect us to meet there. Be there on time, jack-off."

* * *

After Proctor hung up with the dentist, he went up to his room and took a long nap. By the time he woke up, it was dark outside. He only had an hour to get ready for his blind date with the dentist and he didn't have time to soak in the tub. So he showered, shaved his body, and did his hair. He sprayed on his tan, wiped some off, and put on his new black tuxedo. He wasn't doing this to impress the dentist. He could have worn one of his older tuxedos and it wouldn't have mattered. But that night he was going to one of the most elegant, expensive restaurants in Los Angeles and he needed to feel like he was still rich.

When he went downstairs, Jane was standing in the hallway waiting for him. The dentist wasn't picking him up. Proctor had insisted he meet the dentist at the restaurant to make it easier. He said he didn't want Kent to go out of his way. But the real reason he decided to drive his own car was to get away fast if Kent turned out to be a creep.

He glanced at Jane and asked, "Did you feed Constance?" She was a finicky cat. Anyone would think that since she looked so much like a real leopard, she'd eat anything. But she'd only eat the cheapest cat food, in one flavor: ocean whitefish.

Jane nodded. "Yes, everything is taken care of for the night. Are you driving yourself again?" Jane looked as if she was going out, too. She had on a pink dress with white sandals, and a white shawl around her shoulders.

Proctor flung her a look. "Yes, I'm driving myself. I'm getting good at it, too. In fact, I've forgotten how much I like to drive. I should have been doing it more often and not wasting money on drivers." He hated driving. But saying this aloud made him feel better. "Are you going out?" He sighed. Sometimes they were like two old maid sisters living in a Tennessee Williams play.

Jane smiled. "I'm going to bingo at the church."

Before Proctor could reply, the phone rang and Jane reached for it. She nodded a few times, and said, "I'm not sure. Let me check." Then she held her hand over the speaker and glanced at Proctor. "There's a man on the phone who wants to speak to you."

"Who is he? It had better not be that fucking dentist backing out at the last minute. I'll cut his fucking balls off."

Jane smiled again. "It's not the dentist. It's a man with a very aggressive tone. He says his name is Blair Huntingdon and he needs to talk to you about an urgent business matter."

Proctor closed his eyes and took a quick breath. The last person he wanted to speak with was Blair. The idiot had left black and blue bruises on the backs of his legs from the elevator fuck. And there was no way Proctor wanted to discuss keeping that agency open a day longer than he had to. "Tell him I went out."

"I can't lie," Jane said. "I hate to lie."

He knew she was like this. It was one of the qualities about her that he loved most. "Then tell him I'm on my way out and I can't talk. That's the truth. You're not lying."

Jane bit her lip and nodded, as if she had to think about this first. Then she lifted the phone and said, "Mr. Gamble is on his way out and he can't speak. May I take a message?"

Proctor watched as Jane listened.

Then Jane said, "I'm not sure. All I know is he's going to the best restaurant in Los Angeles. That's all I can say."

When Jane hung up, Proctor sighed and said, "And if that man calls again, tell him I'm not home." He hoped Jane hadn't given away too much information about where he was going to dinner. But he didn't want to upset Jane by mentioning this, so he let it go.

"What if you are home?"

Proctor rolled his eyes and frowned. "Tell him the truth. Tell him I don't want to talk to him, not now or ever. But with his type, it's a lot easier to lie, trust me." Then he kissed Jane on the cheek, told her to have fun at bingo, and went out to his car.

When Proctor arrived at the restaurant, Dr. Kent Russell was waiting for him in the lobby. This restaurant was located in one of the most elegant hotels in the city, on the top floor with a view overlooking Los Angeles. Kent wore a black tuxedo with a red carnation, as he'd said he would, so Proctor would recognize him. Kent wasn't bad looking at all, if you went for older guys. He looked more like he was in his mid-60s than 50s, with pure white hair that had violet rinse, shiny skin that looked as if he'd recently had Botox injections, and perfectly tweezed white eyebrows. If there was one thing about a man, gay or straight, that Proctor couldn't abide was perfectly tweezed eyebrows. And if there was one more thing about a man Proctor couldn't abide, it was verbosity.

This one started talking the moment they met, all through the hotel lobby, and all the way up to the top floor. He spoke about a new dental procedure he'd been working on, involving crowns and some sort of new dental cement, and he spoke without using commas or periods. When they finally reached the top floor and the elevator doors opened, he smiled at Proctor and said, "You're so quiet. You haven't said a word about my new treatment."

Proctor glanced at him and forced a half smile. In a deadpan tone, he said, "I'm at a loss for words."

The dentist took this as a compliment. He set his palm on Proctor's back, smiled, and guided him into the restaurant. "I knew you'd be impressed. This procedure will change the tooth business forever."

Proctor wanted to lift his hand and twirl his finger. But he just smiled and nodded, portending this might be one of the longest nights of his life.

They had one of the best tables in the restaurant, with a view that would have been breathtaking if the dentist only knew when to stop talking about teeth. Proctor ordered a salad and said he preferred to eat lightly. Kent ordered four courses, including a massive lobster. When the lobster arrived, Kent put on a bib and went to town with tools and tiny forks. While he cracked, he spoke about teeth. While he ate, he spoke about teeth with his mouth full. While he dipped lobster in drawn butter, he talked about gum disease. He even spoke about teeth while he sipped his martini. Proctor learned how many teeth there were in the human mouth. He learned the differences between taking gas and having Novocain. When the dentist cracked a lobster claw and said he'd named all of his homes "Tooth Acres," he smiled so wide Proctor could see *his* back teeth.

When he finished the lobster, Kent stood up and said he had to go to the rest room to brush and floss. He said he should have done this after the second course, but he'd been too lazy to bother. By that time Proctor was fighting back a yawn. He forced himself to sit up straight, smile, and say, "You go ahead. I think I'll just wait until I get home to brush, thank you."

"I won't be long," Kent said.

Without looking up, Proctor said, "Take your time," in a slow, even tone.

But the minute the dentist walked away, someone placed a hand on Proctor's shoulder and said, "Don't be alarmed. I'm only going to say a few words and then I'll leave."

Proctor turned fast. He saw Blair Huntingdon standing over him. "What are *you* doing here? I told my assistant I didn't want to speak with you tonight. I'm on a date with a very exciting man. Who are you?"

Without being asked, Blair sat down in the dentist's seat and said, "I could see he was exciting by the way you've been turning away, covering your mouth, and yawning all night. You looked absolutely captivated by his magic."

"I'm having a wonderful time," Proctor said. "And how did you find me?"

"I'm a private detective," Blair said. "Duh. I followed you here."

"You were the idiot behind me with those bright lights while I was driving over here tonight."

"I started to worry. You drive so slowly. And the way you almost clipped that milk truck freaked me out. I'm telling you, my nuts were up in my throat all the way over here. Have you been driving for long?"

"So you're a stalker, too."

Blair ignored the stalker comment and glanced down at the table. "I *love* lobster."

"Oh, don't be obtuse."

"I promise I won't be *obtuse* if you promise to *parse*."

"You're an idiot!"

Blair smiled. "I know. That's why you like me."

"I never said I liked you." Proctor felt like throwing a lobster claw at him.

"When your pants were down around your ankles in the elevator, I kind of assumed you liked me. Or do you let men you don't like fuck you that way all the time?"

"What do you want from me?" Proctor wondered how anyone could be so pushy and get away with it.

Blair held up a set of keys. "I just wanted to return the company car in person. I'm a man of my word. I also wanted to tell you I think you're missing out on something big here. You need money. I can help you get money. You're looking at the most sought-after detective in the business. The agency you own is not a shoddy enterprise, by any means. I just need to talk. I've had offers from every single agency in town since you told me you're shutting down. People are begging me, literally pleading with me. I don't want you to miss out on the deal of a lifetime, is all."

Although Proctor wasn't in the mood for this, he had to admit it was the first time all night he felt like smiling. Blair talked too much, too, but at least he had something to say and it wasn't about teeth. There was something about the way Blair smiled while he spoke that was fascinating to watch. And although he was almost as long winded as the dentist, at least the corners of his lips turned up in a cute, adorable way. But Proctor said, "If you're not gone in 30 seconds, I'm going to call the police." He pulled his iPhone out of his breast pocket and dialed a nine.

This didn't intimidate Blair. He smiled even wider and said, "I guess that will get your attention. I'll bet the good dentist will come running back with dental floss stuck between his teeth to save you and sweep you off your feet."

"How do you know Kent is a dentist?" Blair shrugged. "Kent. What a quaint name. I know the head waiter here. Your date is a regular. This is where he brings all his paid male escorts." He leaned forward and gazed into Proctor's eyes without blinking. "Tell me, how is this date working out for you? I hear from a good source the good dentist wears thong underwear and he pops Viagra while he's in the restroom flossing so he'll be prepared for what's to come later. Tell me, are you going to let him get into your hot little pants tonight? Or are you going to play hard to get, like you did with me in the elevator this afternoon?"

Proctor put his phone back in his pocket and stood up. He threw his napkin on the table and said, "I've had it. If you won't leave, I will. I don't need to be insulted anymore."

Blair followed him to the other restroom out in the main restaurant lobby. Proctor didn't want to run into the dentist while he was flossing in the other one. When they reached the men's room door, Blair grabbed Proctor's wrist and said, "I just need to talk this over with you. You're making a huge mistake and I'm trying to help."

Proctor jerked sideways. "There's nothing to talk about. And I don't see how you're going to help me. You can't even help yourself."

Blair's face fell. He stopped smiling and his body relaxed. "I think you need me, and I know I need you. I'm going to be honest this time. No jokes, no games, no fast talk. This job was the best thing that ever happened to me. I come from a poor background. I was kicked out of the house at s16 because they found out I was gay. I took a bus to L.A., never looked back, and managed to survive on next to nothing. I got my GED and worked my way through community college studying criminal justice, doing anything I could to do to make enough money to eat. I did it legally, too. I've never broken a law in my life. I've never harmed anyone in my life. Just give me a chance. I can make this work. Please reconsider."

This was almost more than Proctor could stand. When he looked into Blair's eyes, his chest caved in and he wanted to hug him. He'd always admired people who'd learned how to survive the hard way. His own life hadn't been easy either. But he wasn't in a position to help anyone. His situation was as bad as Blair's. "The only thing I need is a good modeling job right now," Proctor said. Then he turned toward the men's room, praying Blair wouldn't follow him, without glancing back at Blair's desperate and adorable expression.

* * *

On the other side of town, the barefoot jogger hopped into a 20 year old Jeep, with dented doors and faded gray paint. He'd just fucked the guy in his bed one more time and his dick was still wet. He didn't bother to shower. He put on his faded old jeans, an old black T-shirt, and a pair of heavy black boots with thick heels, without socks. The only thing he wanted to do that night was meet Morris at the fancy restaurant.

29

He drove fast through town, in and out of traffic. He'd stopped worrying about the police a long time ago. There was nothing they could do to him but put him in jail overnight. He didn't have a license, insurance, or registration. A night in jail would mean a few solid meals, a good hot shower, and clean clothes. If he was lucky, he'd find a sweet set of lips willing to suck him off before he went to sleep. He'd been to prison before; he'd been a huge hit there with cocksuckers.

When he reached a traffic light that wasn't far from the restaurant, he slowed to a stop next to an older model Honda Civic that looked even worse than his Jeep. He revved the engine and lit a cigarette. Then he noticed a large black Cadillac behind him with blinking lights. He felt a rush of adrenaline and his heart began to race. He knew they were after him. Morris drove a white Lincoln. It wasn't Morris. He'd been followed.

He didn't want to get caught.

So before the light changed, he lifted the clutch, hit the gas, and turned to the left. There were construction cones and barriers on the dark empty street. He jumped the sidewalk, slithered between the cones, and jerked back onto the pavement. But when he reached the middle of the street, a big yellow dump truck backed up and forced him to stop. A second later, the black Cadillac pulled up beside him, trapping him there with no way out. The Cadillac had dark tinted windows and he couldn't see who was inside. He felt his face getting warmer and his legs started to tingle. When he glanced at the Cadillac, the rear window went down halfway and a man with dark hair said, "I'd like you to please pull over."

The barefoot jogger panicked. He spoke too fast. "Leave me alone." He had to figure a way out of this fast.

The driver climbed out of the Cadillac and crossed in front of the Jeep. While he leaned into the window on the driver's side, the man with dark hair climbed out of the backseat and walked to the passenger side.

The dark-haired man bent down and said, "All I'm asking is that we chat. I know you have the ring and I need it. I know the man you work for wants it badly. But I want it just as much. I was hoping we could negotiate and make a deal that works out for both of us. You seem like a nice young man. I wouldn't want to see anything happen to you."

The barefoot jogger looked forward and backward. He was pinned, with nowhere to go. He gripped the steering wheel so his hands wouldn't shake and he said, "Leave me alone. Get away from me."

As the man with dark hair reached for the handle to open the door, the yellow dump truck moved forward, leaving a small open space for the barefoot jogger to slip through. If he hit the gas now, he knew he could make it. So he took a deep breath, lifted the clutch, and sped forward.

The two men jumped into the Cadillac and followed him around a wide corner. He saw them in the distance through the rear-view mirror. He almost slammed into a small convertible backing out of a parking garage. The barefoot jogger didn't have a choice. He had to keep moving. If they got him, he knew what would happen. The best thing he could hope for now was that a cop would pull him over. At least he'd be safe.

* * *

At the restaurant, Proctor poked his head through the restroom door and looked around for Blair Huntingdon. When he didn't see him, he squared his shoulders and headed to his table. But the moment he entered the lobby, Blair crept up behind him and said, "Have you been listening to me at all?"

Proctor jumped. He turned and said, "Are you trying to give me a heart attack? Leave me alone." Then he turned and headed to his table.

Blair refused to leave. "The least you can do is listen to me. I came all the way over here, paid a fucking fortune to park, took a shower, and trimmed my nuts just to look good for you."

"Oh, thank you for that information. I can sleep so much better tonight knowing you manscaped." Actually, he thought it was cute that he'd trimmed his nuts. But he didn't want Blair to know this.

"*Manscaped*?"

Proctor sighed. "Forget about it."

Blair reached for his arm. "I'm just trying to talk to you. I'm not trying to get into your pants."

"Good, because you're not getting into my pants again."

"Then shut up and listen to me."

If this was the only way to get rid of him, Proctor figured he would listen. He turned and said, "Okay, talk to me. You have two minutes."

Blair took a deep breath and exhaled, as if he were about to go on stage and give a speech. "I know what you're dealing with. You're having financial problems and I know I can help. This agency is a money maker."

31

"But you've been losing money for years," Proctor said, laughing in his face.

Blair's eyebrows went up. "That's because I was supposed to lose money. But I'm sure I can make money."

"You're wasting your time and my time," Proctor said, as he turned toward his table.

"I'm good at what I do," Blair said. "I'm the best in the business."

"Then why were you *losing* money?"

Blair smacked the heel of his palm to his forehead. "I was *supposed* to lose money so you'd have something to write off at tax time. I was good at losing money. But I have the experience and the training to make money. All I need is one big case, and with you I'm sure I can get it. You're a huge celebrity. You're one of the most beautiful men in the world, and I'm not just blowing smoke up your sweet ass either. With that kind of exposure, it's a win-win for both of us."

Proctor sat down and sighed. "Have a good night, Mr. Huntingdon. We're finished talking." He wasn't going to let this sweet-talking con man sway his opinion. He'd already been cheated enough in the last month.

Then Kent returned to the table with the lobster bib still around his neck and a toothbrush in his right hand. He smiled at Blair and looked down at Proctor. "I'm sorry. I have to leave. I had a phone call while I was flossing. It's a dental emergency."

Proctor wanted to club the old fool with a lobster claw. He'd been hoping Kent would save him from Blair.

But Blair leaned forward and said, "It's nice to meet you, doc. I'm Blair Huntingdon. I'm a business associate of Mr. Gamble's. We work very closely together. I'm here with my wife and kids tonight." He leaned forward and waved at a group of strange people on the other side of the restaurant. They all waved back.

Proctor turned in the direction of his fake wave and blinked. The guy was an artist.

Blair said, "But since you have to leave, I guess you won't be able to join us."

"I'm going to leave now, too," Proctor said. He smiled at Kent and tried to get up. "I'll go with you."

"Nonsense," Blair said. "You can join us."

Kent smiled and patted Proctor on the shoulder. "I can see you're in good hands."

Blair smiled. "You have no idea how good my hands are."

Proctor shot Blair a glare. He had no intention of having sex with him ever again. He was sorry he'd done it once.

Kent turned to leave. He kissed Proctor on the cheek. "I'm sorry about the emergency. But it can't be helped. I took care of the check. I'll call you."

When he was gone, Proctor stood up and turned his back on Blair.

Blair said, "I guess we can get back to business now that Dr. Thong is gone."

"I'm going home. You're out of a job and I'm tired. There's nothing to talk about."

They walked through the restaurant, with Blair a few feet behind Proctor. Blair continued talking, selling his detective skills and pointing out all the good things that would happen if Proctor changed his mind and kept the agency open. When they reached the elevator and stopped to wait for the doors to open, Blair stood behind Proctor. While no one was watching, he gently put his hand on Proctor's ass and said, "At least let me follow you home so I know you got back okay. I hate the thought of you driving through the dark Los Angeles streets at this time of night."

Blair gritted his teeth. "Get your hand off my ass."

Blair squeezed harder and said, "I know you like it. Why fight it?"

Before Proctor had a chance to reply, the elevator doors opened and a strange young man with heavy black boots with thick heels, worn jeans that looked as if they hadn't been laundered in weeks, and a black T-shirt stood there staring at them. There were tattoos all over his arms and several of his facial features had been pierced. His eyes were wide open and his lips clamped shut.

Proctor's stomach jumped and he took a step back. The odd young guy didn't move left or right. He just stood there staring at Proctor, with his jaws locked, as if unable to speak.

When Proctor said, "Pardon me," the guy opened his mouth and pulled out a large gold ring.

"This one's a real creep," Blair said. "And he could use a shower. He smells like ass. Do you know him well?"

"Of course I don't know him," said Proctor. "And don't be so crude."

The guy reached for Proctor's hand and tried to put the ring on his finger.

"No, thanks," Proctor said. "The only jewelry I wear is a watch. I prefer things simple. I've never been big on rings or showy gold chains, thank you."

Blair laughed. "I think he's asking for your hand in marriage. You're not getting any younger, you know. You might want to think it over."

"Don't just stand there making stupid jokes, you idiot, do something," Proctor said.

Blair shrugged. "*What can I do? He's in love.*"

The tattooed guy held Proctor's wrist tighter, while Proctor continued to protest, until the ring was on Proctor's finger. The only other person in the restaurant who seemed to be paying attention to them was an older man with thin white hair, wearing a brown tweed blazer. Proctor noticed him from the corner of his eye, standing behind a small group of people near the elevator. For a moment, he hoped the old guy would come over and do something since Blair obviously wasn't going to do anything.

Proctor gaped at the ring on his finger and looked up in horror. It was the ugliest ring he'd ever seen, with a slightly raised buffalo on the top. The guy's body began to sway left, then right, as if he couldn't keep his balance. "What the fuck is wrong with him, Blair?" Proctor asked.

Blair shrugged. "Too many olives?"

A second later, the guy lurched forward and fell flat on his face. When Proctor looked down and saw the knife sticking out of his back and blood dripping down his jeans, he smacked his palm to his chest, his eyes rolled back, and he collapsed into Blair's arms.

Chapter Four

The police brought Proctor and Blair downtown to question them both about the guy who had been stabbed in the elevator. They escorted Proctor into the interrogation room first, asked him basic questions, and treated him with care. He was polite and he smiled the entire time. Proctor told them the truth: he knew nothing about the guy or the stabbing, and said he wasn't in any way connected with the incident. He expressed genuine surprise when they told him the young guy who had been stabbed was named Rolf Braun. When he told them the reason he'd gone to the restaurant had to do with his attorney setting him up on the most awful blind date he'd ever experienced, the police asked for the dentist's contact information so they could back his story up and said it wouldn't be necessary for Proctor to phone his attorney yet. Proctor knew what he was doing. The police didn't seem comfortable talking about his blind date with a man or that he was openly gay. They couldn't wait to get rid of him.

The police checked out his story with the dentist, then released him to the waiting room. They asked him to wait there for a few minutes and took Blair Huntingdon into the interrogation room next. Proctor figured the police wanted to check his story against Blair's.

He wound up waiting for almost two hours, hoping Blair wouldn't say the wrong thing and get them both into more trouble than they were already in. Blair talked so fast and said so many outrageous, unbelievable things that didn't make sense, Proctor worried the police might consider him a liar and a prime suspect. At one point, when Proctor saw a delivery man carry huge bags of Chinese take-out into the interrogation room, he gritted his teeth and kicked the side of his chair. When he overheard Blair say, "It's on me, guys. I'm paying," he dug his fingernails into the arm of the chair so hard he left marks. While Proctor sat and waited alone, wearing a tuxedo, in a room full of criminal types who hadn't showered

35

in days, Blair was in there entertaining the police with his charm and wit. And he was doing it at Proctor's expense, no doubt, with agency money. He'd probably paid for the Chinese take-out with a company credit card.

When they finally did release Blair, he swaggered out of the interrogation room with his cocky head up and his shoulders squared. He wiped a noodle from his chin with a small paper napkin and said, "Looks like we're all done here for now, baby."

There were two policemen with him. They were both eating egg rolls, dabbing their chins. Proctor stood up and frowned at Blair. He felt like wiping the snide grin off his face. "Don't call me baby." He turned to the cops. "I'm not his baby."

The cops exchanged glances and rolled their eyes.

Blair set his palm on the small of Proctor's back. "Don't be shy, baby. I already told them all about you. That you're my new business partner and you're a little uncomfortable about being openly gay." He turned to the police and winked. "He's really a sweetheart once you get to know him. Don't pay attention to the bad attitude."

The cops exchanged uncomfortable glances again and swallowed egg roll at the same time, as if they weren't sure how to respond.

"I'll have you know I was the first openly gay male model to come out in public," Proctor said. "I've never hidden who I was."

Blair smiled and said, "Now, don't get mad, baby. I'm only trying to help you out."

Proctor took a deep breath and exhaled. He glanced at the cops and said, "Is there anything else you need from me? I'd like to go home."

A tall cop wiped egg roll from his chin and said, "We just need you to sign a police report, nothing serious. Mr. Huntingdon has already signed. Then you're free to go."

"Thank you," Proctor said. He scowled at Blair. "You have no idea what a night this has been for me. I'd like to go home now… *alone.*"

"If you'll follow me," the tall cop said.

As the tall cop led him out toward a large open office, Proctor turned and followed. He overheard Blair tell the other cop, "He's really a great guy, seriously. He's just a little freaked out right now. See the way he's walking, as if he has a big stick up his ass. That's only stress. Once he limbers up a little, he's a lot more fun."

Proctor stopped and turned around. He glared at Blair for a moment without saying a word. He'd taken his tuxedo jacket off and he knew

Blair was staring at his ass. He could tell by the sly grin on Blair's face and the lewd twinkle in his eyes.

Blair pursed his lips and whistled back. "Look at the way his pants pull across the seat: tight, hard, firm." He bit his bottom lip and leaned into the other cop. "Not too bad, though, huh?"

The cop blinked and turned sideways. Evidently, he wasn't used to checking out other guys' butts.

Proctor rolled his eyes, turned, and left Blair standing there without saying a word. If he said something, it would only encourage the moron to make more obnoxious remarks about his ass. At the same time, even though he wanted to kick Blair in the ass, he couldn't help enjoying the compliment or the way Blair was making the homophobic cops squirm without being too obvious. Blair wasn't dumb.

Signing the police report took another 20 minutes. It was the typical red tape and government nonsense that everyone expects from staffers who don't really like what they do for a living. When they finally released Proctor, he put on his jacket and exited through the main door of the station. He didn't see Blair anywhere; he figured he'd finally left him alone. He glanced at his watch and sighed. It was after 3:00 AM in the morning and he'd left his car in the hotel parking garage. He decided he'd wait until he was outside to call a taxi. He needed fresh air. He didn't want to call Jane and wake her in the middle of the night. He would send someone to get his car tomorrow.

As he pulled the station doors open, about the same exact moment he was ready to take a deep breath, people started shouting and yelling his name. There were photographers, journalists, and a few local television stations. He felt like turning back and running away. But it was too late; he knew he had to stand there and smile so the public wouldn't think there was anything wrong. The only other thought going through his mind was how the press had found out about this so soon. It wasn't as if he were still a huge celebrity. He made headlines on occasion, but not for anything considered important. He figured this must be a slow news week. If something more important had been going on, he wouldn't have had to suffer this ordeal on top of everything else he'd been through that week.

So he squared his back and turned up his lips. The moment he stepped outside, a pushy woman shoved a microphone in his face and said, "Mr. Gamble, we'd like to ask you a few questions." She turned toward the camera. "This is Gayle Kline of *Good Morning, Los Angeles*, and we're standing outside a Los Angeles police station where Proctor Gamble was being held for questioning regarding the Rolf Braun murder, and has just been released. Proctor Gamble is well known for his famous poster for the Exotique Underwear Company, which broke record number for the most posters ever sold, since the famous Farrah Fawcett swimsuit poster in the 1970s." She turned to Proctor and held the microphone higher. "Mr. Gamble, you are denying any involvement with the alleged murder of Rolf Braun."

There were bright lights and Proctor's eyes began to sting. He shielded his eyes and said, "I'm sorry. Can't you turn those lights the other way? I can't see anything." He'd learned, through years of experience, that it was always safer to avoid any direct answers with the press and change the subject without being too obvious. Anything he said would be quoted, and most likely be misinterpreted.

The reporter continued to push. "Is it true that you and your business partner, a Mr. Blair Huntingdon, have just opened a new private investigation agency and that your first case will involve the alleged murder of Rolf Braun?"

When Proctor heard this, he turned to the reporter and glared. "What did Mr. Huntingdon tell you?"

In the background, beyond the large group of reporters and TV cameras, Proctor heard a loud whistle. Then he heard Blair Huntingdon cheering and applauding. No one else paid attention to him. But Proctor glanced over their heads, focused in Blair's silly grin, and said, "You'd better stick around, because someone else might get killed tonight." He wanted to yank Blair by the back of the neck, swing him around, and send him sailing into the Los Angeles harbor. He must have been the one who called the press and tipped them off.

As Proctor was about to step down so he could grab Blair and set all this straight in front of the press, he watched Blair turn and run across the street. Proctor shoved his way through the crowd, past the reporters, and followed him around a dark corner into a parking garage that was part of the police station. The press followed him for a moment, but stopped when they saw he wasn't going to cooperate with them. When Proctor walked inside, down a low concrete ramp, the parking garage was dark and quiet. There were marked vehicles and a few dark cars and SUVs Proctor assumed were unmarked police cars.

He set his jaw and said, "Blair, I know you're in here. I'm going to strangle you for what you just did. I've never been so mad in my life. I've always managed to stay out of the press."

No one answered; there was dead silence except for a screeching car on the street.

"You can't hide from me," Proctor said. "I'll find you and I'll get even no matter how long it takes." He clenched his fists and shouted this time: "*Blair.*"

A voice rang out from behind a black and white police car about 15 feet away. "He's not in here."

Proctor crossed to the police car and started to scream. "I don't want any fucking contact with you again. Do you understand? Leave me alone."

Blair stood slowly, with his arms up, and said, "Don't be unreasonable. Don't do anything you'll be sorry for."

"I'm serious," Proctor said. "I've had it with you. You're ruining my life, or what's left of my life. Get the fuck away from me." He felt his face getting hotter. His stomach started to pull and he felt lightheaded. He wasn't used to this kind of excitement. He lived a quiet, privileged, ordinary life. He liked things simple and organized. He took a deep breath and lowered his voice. "I can't believe you called the press and told them those things."

Blair shrugged and smiled. "No need to thank me for doing you a favor. It's a great show, and people love Gayle Kline. There are a lot of important people on her show. You could use the exposure."

When he said this, Proctor smacked his head and leaned forward. He set his palms on the hood of the police car and said, "A young man was stabbed to death tonight. He died in front of me. This is serious."

Blair considered this for a moment, then said, "Ah well."

When Proctor saw no concern in Blair's eyes, he turned around slowly, leaned up against the police car, and folded his arms across his chest. He felt a sting in his eyes and he didn't want to cry in front of Blair. Proctor had never seen a dead person before, let alone been that close to one. When he thought about the magnitude of all this, he felt completely overwhelmed.

Blair adjusted his shoulders and slowly walked around to where he was leaning. He stood in front of Proctor and set both hands on Proctor's waist. He lowered his voice and said, "I'm an asshole. You have every

39

right to be mad at me. I didn't think about you once. I'm nothing but a selfish prick who only cares about himself and no one else."

Proctor didn't reply. He stood there, staring at the exit, with no expression at all. Deep down, though he would never admit this aloud, he wanted to smile at the way Blair was groveling now.

Blair leaned forward and kissed him on the cheek. "All I can say is I'm very sorry for what I've put you through and I'm going to leave you alone forever."

Proctor remained silent. He knew he was in control now that he knew Blair actually had a soft side.

"I'm serious," Blair said. "I'm going to turn around and leave right now." Instead of turning, he took a small step forward and kissed Proctor on the cheek again.

When Proctor felt Blair's warm breath on his neck, he slowly lifted his arms and kissed Proctor on the lips. Though he'd vowed he'd never have sex with Blair again, the feelings that had been building deep down inside were too strong to control. His pants grew tighter and his heart raced. Blair didn't waste a moment; he seized the opportunity. He fell into Proctor's body, slid his tongue into Proctor's mouth, and reached down to unfasten Proctor's pants.

They moved even faster now than they'd moved in the elevator. Their arms and hands moved in all directions. They kissed so hard and so deep it was hard to catch a breath. The parking garage was dark and quiet, but still slightly dangerous because anyone could walk in on them at any moment. With Proctor's pants down around his knees, while they continued to kiss, Blair pulled him to a dark corner and shoved him into another empty police car.

Proctor didn't resist when Blair removed his jacket. He liked the way Blair's strong hands felt against his body. They made him feel both dangerous and safe at the same time, which was something no man had ever been able to do for him. He felt sexy, too, which is something he hadn't felt in a long time. The way Blair held him and caressed him caused his dick to grow so hard it brought him to the thin line between pain and pleasure.

When Blair pulled down his pants and kissed his naked thighs, he didn't put up a fight. He kicked off his shoes so Blair could remove his pants and his socks without struggling. Then he pulled his shirt over his head and tossed it over his shoulder. He didn't know where it landed and he didn't care. He wanted to be naked. He wanted Blair to take him on his back this time so he could see Blair's expression while they fucked.

The chemistry between them that night was so strong it seemed as if Blair could read his mind. When Proctor was naked, Blair grabbed his waist and hoisted him up to the hood of the car. Then Blair pulled a condom out of his back pocket. He unzipped his pants, opened his belt, and dropped his pants and boxer shorts to his knees. While he covered his dick with the condom, Proctor reached down and cupped Blair's balls so he could see if Blair had really shaved them that night.

Blair said, "Oooh, baby. That feels so good. I like the way you touch me. You have great hands."

Proctor smiled and squeezed his balls tighter. Although he was always the alleged submissive with men, this always gave him such a strong sense of control. These balls were, indeed, soft and warm, without a hint of pubic hair. "I just wanted to be sure you weren't lying to me about shaving your balls."

Blair leaned back and spread his legs wider. "I'd never lie to you about my nuts."

When Blair said this, he smiled. He looked into Proctor's eyes and they both remained still for a moment. A sharp jolt of emotion passed through Proctor's entire body. A moment after that, Blair pushed him back against the cold hood of the police car and told him to lift his legs. He said, "I'm gonna fuck your brains out, baby." Then he moved between Proctor's legs and rubbed the head of his dick around Proctor's opening. He did this with furrowed eyebrows, gazing down between Proctor's legs. His lips remained pursed, as if he were fascinated by what he saw down there.

The moment of penetration was swift and unforgiving. Blair plunged deeply, without taking his time. Proctor's head went back; so did his arms and all of his dreams of finding peace and quiet that night. With his legs bent at the knee, he spread them as wide as he could and arched his back so Blair wouldn't have to work hard to get to the bottom of his ass. When he did this, Blair grabbed the tops of his thighs tightly and started fucking with short strides. He fucked deeply, with a quick tempo, and pulled Proctor's ass into his pelvis each time he slammed. Proctor pointed his toes and moaned. They ignored the sounds of cars on the street. They didn't stop fucking when someone on the other side of the garage whistled a tuneless song and slammed a door.

By the time Proctor's legs were dangling over Blair's forearms, Blair was fucking him so hard and so fast there were beads of perspiration trickling down his cheeks. His face turned red, his cheeks puffed out, and he started to grunt. The faster he fucked, the more he grunted. The more he grunted the more he perspired. Proctor reached down and took his own dick; he knew they would climax soon. As he started jerking, he looked into Blair's eyes and nodded. Then, in a low voice, he said, "Come inside me."

This time Blair blasted his load with such power he slammed into Proctor's ass, his pelvis went forward, and he stood on his tiptoes as if he couldn't get in deeply enough. His head went back and his jaw dropped. He let out a deep sound that came from the bottom of his diaphragm. While his chest heaved, he remained this way for a long time. Proctor reached for Blair's right hand with his left. Blair was still holding his thighs, pulling him as close as he could. Proctor set his palm on top of Blair's hand and felt a jolt of energy. He squeezed Blair's hand hard, as if holding on for his life, and jacked out his own load with his other hand. It went up in an arc, shot through the air, and landed splat in the middle of police car windshield. When Proctor released his dick and took a breath, Blair leaned forward and grabbed the back of his neck. He pulled Proctor's face toward his, remaining deep inside. He held him tightly, kissed him one last time, and whispered, "Damn, that was hot. Thanks."

Proctor caressed the back of his head and said, "I have to get dressed now. Pull out."

Blair slapped his ass and said, "What the fuck just happened here? I think we made love again."

"A lot of people wouldn't think this is very romantic," Proctor said.

Blair slapped his ass again. "Fuck 'em. A lot of people never get to experience what I just did to you."

Proctor laughed. Blair could be smug. He lifted his leg, set his bare foot on Blair's chest, and pushed him backward. When Blair exited his body, he felt a strange sense of emptiness that caused a sudden feeling of despair. He glanced down and smiled at the way Blair's condom covered dick dangled between his legs. Then he hopped down from the hood and said, "Nothing happened here of any significance. We just fucked. Don't get the wrong idea." Proctor wanted Blair to understand this wasn't going to change anything between them. He'd once heard an old saying that two drowning men can't save each other. And Proctor needed someone with a life preserver, not a cute smile and a great dick.

While Proctor searched for his pants, Blair pulled his up and said, "You're such a sweet little thing. I love the way you want to cuddle in my big, strong, manly arms."

Proctor put on his socks and pulled up his pants. "Grow up, idiot. We're both men, not ladies. This isn't a Lifetime movie for women." With the right man, Proctor loved to cuddle in bed. But he had to be strong. A man like Blair Huntingdon would only bring him down and make his life more miserable than it already was.

Blair removed the condom and tossed it into a dark corner. He zipped up his pants and said, "Do I at least get to walk you to your door tonight and kiss you goodnight?"

Proctor crossed to the other side of the police car to find his shirt. He put it on fast, tucked it into his pants, and said, "It's time for you to leave."

"You don't mean that. Not after what just happened."

"Oh yes, I do, buddy." He tied his shoes and adjusted his socks.

"You know, I think I've had just about enough insults from you for one night. I do all these wonderful things for you, including give you the best poke you've ever had, and this is how you repay me. Why don't you just kick me in the ass while you're at it?"

Proctor shot him a glare. "Don't tempt me. Besides, you don't know that was the best *poke*, as you so eloquently refer to sex, I've ever had. Your ego is as big as your mouth. You're a narcissist."

Blair smiled. "Oh, I know you liked it. I could see the way you were bending and moving. In fact, I've never seen anyone spread their legs so wide before, man or woman. And I've had plenty of both. I thought you were going to howl like an alley cat."

Proctor adjusted his belt and said, "The only thing I want now is for you to leave. It was nice knowing you, but now it's time for you to get out of my life forever."

"I left my car keys with a friend at the restaurant," Blair said. "He brought my car over here and left it outside on the street. He hid the keys under the tire. I'll take you home."

He seemed to have friends and connections all over town. Proctor turned his back and started walking in the opposite direction. "I have my phone. I'll call a taxi." He didn't look back. He had a feeling Blair's head was down and he was pouting with that adorable expression that could tug at his heart.

"I'm leaving now," Blair said. "I'm serious. You're not going to have me around to kick much longer."

Proctor continued walking to a doorway where there was a small light coming from an exit sign so he could see his phone. "So long."

"I'm not joking," Blair said. "I'm really leaving this time."

Proctor waved over his shoulder. "Have a good night, sweetie."

By the time Proctor reached the doorway, he turned to see if Blair was still there. He almost sighed when he saw he'd left. But it was better this way. So he pulled his phone out and started to dial the taxi company. He kept this number on speed dial just in case. But when a voice answered on the other end of the line, a bright red custom BMW sports car plowed into the parking lot, sped to the other side, and turned around with a loud screech. It fishtailed a few times before it regained its balance. Then the car sped up to the door where Proctor was standing and stopped short.

Proctor shut off his phone and put it back in his pocket. When the passenger window went down, he leaned forward and looked into the car.

Blair smiled and said, "Get in. I'll take you home. I'm not leaving you here alone."

"I told you I'm fine. Just go."

Blair climbed out of the car and said, "It's your car. You may as well take advantage of it."

This made Proctor think twice. It *was* his car and he had every right to drive it home. Why should he take a taxi? Let the idiot con man take a taxi. So he walked around Blair, sat down behind the steering wheel, and put on his seatbelt.

Blair leaned into the open window on the passenger side. "I couldn't leave you here in this dark dangerous place, where anything could happen. You're much too gentle and sweet." He smiled and tapped the door, waiting for Proctor to invite him to get into the car. "Yes, this is a dangerous place, where I now have to stay alone, with no means of transportation, where anything can happen to me."

When Proctor heard the gentle, sarcastic tone in his voice, he grabbed the steering wheel and thought for a moment. He took a breath and exhaled, then turned to Blair and said, "Okay, get in. But I don't want to hear a single word out of you. This is quiet time. No talking while I drive. I like peace and calm at all times."

Blair got in and put on his seatbelt. "I've seen you drive. I'll just sit here and pray."

Chapter Five

"I could have walked here faster, baby," Blair said, as they pulled through the large electronic gates that would lead them back to Proctor's secluded home in the Hollywood Hills.

"Oh, stop complaining," Proctor said. "I'm a careful driver. I don't speed. And stop calling me baby. I'm not your baby, or anyone else's." He was planning to get out and let Blair take the car home from there. His feet ached, his head pounded, and his stomach growled from not having enough to eat. The first thing he wanted to do when he went into the house was make a sandwich. He'd picked up this glorious piece of his favorite salami in West Hollywood and he couldn't wait to dig in to it that night. The second thing he wanted was to take a long, hot shower before he went to bed. He knew the bottoms of his feet had to be dirty from walking around naked in the police parking garage. He wondered what on Earth had motivated him to get naked and let Blair fuck him again. It was as if this uncontrollable urge overtook him and assaulted all of his good, old-fashioned common sense.

Blair covered his lips with his hand and spoke in a low mumble that was hard to understand. "You drive like my grand mom."

"What was that?" Proctor knew what he said. He wanted him to repeat it, louder.

"I said this is grand house. I love it." He laughed and said, "Who can turn the world on with her smile?"

Proctor knew Blair was joking now. Proctor lived in a home that had been built to resemble the big old house on the *The Mary Tyler Moore Show*. Blair had just recited the first line from the show's theme song. Blair obviously recognized the house. Proctor sent Blair a smile and said, "Certainly not you."

Blair gazed up at the house and scratched his chin. "Tell me, do I get to meet Rhoda and Phyllis and Mr. Grant tonight, or are you saving them for later?"

45

"Very funny, Blair," Proctor said. "The guy who built it was connected with the TV show somehow. That part is sketchy to me. He built the place hidden way back here for his secret gay lover. You know how Hollywood is always covering up those things. I suppose I could find out if I dug deeply enough. But I don't really care. The minute I saw the house I knew I had to have it. It's my sanctuary, and it's also why I have to close down the agency. I don't want to lose this place."

"You're not going to lose the house," Blair said. "You just have to trust me."

Proctor parked up front and climbed out without saying goodnight. Blair met him at the front of the car and set his palm on the small of his back. "What are you doing?" Proctor asked. He wanted to set things straight up front so there were no mistakes. They weren't going to fool around again. He was closing the agency and there was nothing Blair could do to change his mind.

"I'm walking you to the door," Blair said. "I want to make sure you get in okay. Is it a crime to care about you?"

Proctor turned and headed toward the house. The only thing he cared about was his big salami in the refrigerator. If he thought about it long enough, his mouth would water. "I'm a big boy. You can take the car back to wherever you live tonight, then phone me in the morning with an address and I'll have it picked up tomorrow."

Blair's hand went down and rested on Proctor's ass. "Thank you. You're a real sweetheart."

Proctor stopped short. He clenched his fists. "Get your hand off my ass." Good thing he wasn't holding the big salami now. He'd smack him upside the head with it.

Blair stepped away, with both hands up. "Are you kidding me, man? I just fucked your brains out less than an hour ago. You didn't seem to mind me *tagging* your ass on top of a police car."

Proctor flung him a glare. He wasn't in the mood for this. "That's because I gave you permission back there. I didn't give you permission to grab my ass now."

"Oh, I see. I didn't know I needed an invitation to get into your pants. I'm sorry. Next time I'll be sure to ask first. I'll be sure to curtsy, too."

Proctor turned to unlock the front door. "There won't be a next time, so get that out of your head for good. After tonight, the odds are we'll never see each other again."

"I'm getting the feeling you still don't like me, even after all I've done for you," Blair said.

Proctor sighed and lowered his tone. "Give me a break, buddy. I used to be a lot nicer than this. I recently found out my business manager took almost everything I own. I've lost almost all of my employees. I've been running around town trying to sell or close businesses I didn't even know I owned. I've had to fire nice, good people for the first time in my life. I watched a man die in front of me tonight. I've never seen the inside of a police station before tonight. And the person who thinks he's my new business partner called me a *cunt*. I've been having a bad day that doesn't ever end. And now I'd like to go into my home, open a full bottle of vodka, and finish the whole thing." He decided not the mention the salami. Blair would probably start making penis jokes and he wasn't in the mood.

Blair smiled and tilted his head to the side, taking on an innocent quality that almost made Proctor smile. "I can't tell you how good it makes me feel to see you are so willing to share your feelings and emotions with me like that. I almost want to call you sweetie. I feel warm and fuzzy all over, like I just found a basket full of kitties, or I just read a tasteful BDSM book that is filled with more emotion than sex. I feel honored and privileged to have experienced this in my lifetime. I doubt many men have."

That time Proctor almost smiled at his quick, facetious wit. In some ways, he was adorable. In many ways, Proctor agreed with him. But this didn't mean Proctor wanted to get to know him better. "You're an idiot. Now get lost before you ruin any more of my wonderful life."

Then Proctor turned, inserted the key, and opened the front door. As he stepped inside, he heard Blair say, "You're not going to believe this, baby."

"I told you to stop calling me *baby*."

"You're not going to believe this, *bitch*."

Proctor didn't turn around. He had a feeling that if he did, Blair would be standing there with his dick hanging out of his pants, trying to seduce him again. "What now?" There were some men who never knew when to leave.

Blair said, "There's a big blond giant standing behind me poking a gun up against my spine."

Proctor blinked, then turned and saw a huge blond man, with a large crooked nose and small beady eyes, standing right behind Blair. The blond guy wore a well-tailored business suit and a large diamond in his left year. Before Proctor could utter a word, someone crept up behind him from inside the house, wrapped an arm around his neck, and popped a switchblade. When Proctor glanced down and noticed the switchblade only inches from his throat, his knees began to wobble and he felt lightheaded.

The two intruders led Blair and Proctor into the living room. Proctor guessed they must have been professional crooks because they'd found a way to get through his state-of-the-art security system without sounding the alarm. And Jane was probably sound asleep in the guest cottage; she'd never know what was going on in the main house. The tall blond man shoved Blair in first. The one holding the knife to Proctor's throat turned him around and they followed the blond man. The guy with the knife seemed to be the one giving the orders. He wore a dark suit also, and he was about 10 years older than the blond man. His hair was short, thin on top, and dark brown graying at the temples. And though he seemed to be in charge, he spoke with a low, even voice that stopped short of a whimsical stage whisper almost cartoon-like.

When they were in the living room, they sat Blair and Proctor down on the sofa and the blond man went into the kitchen for something. He handed the guy with dark hair his gun before he left, and the guy with dark hair pointed it at Blair and Proctor. While they waited for the blond guy to return from the kitchen, Proctor said a small prayer that Blair would keep his big mouth shut. The last thing he needed was for Blair to get these two thugs pissed off. By that time, Proctor was ready to hand over anything they wanted. He'd gladly give them his jewelry, his watches, his best crystal, and all the technology devices he owned. He'd even give them his beloved salami. The only thing he wanted to do now was go to bed and sleep until Christmas.

The blond guy was only gone a few minutes. When he returned, he took the gun from the dark-haired guy and kept it pointed at Blair and Proctor. The guy with dark hair started to pace the room. He said, in the same low, peculiar voice, "I believe in being up front at all times. I'd like you both to know a little about me, so we don't waste any time. People sometimes refer to me as the Prince. This is my assistant, Garth. But I'm only a simple, quiet entrepreneur, just like the guy who owns the flower shop in West Hollywood and the woman who owns the little café on *Melrose Place*. I'm interested in one thing: making a profit. And just like other businesspeople, there's nothing I won't do to make a profit." He paced a few more times in silence, then asked, "Are you getting it? It's very important that you *get* it."

Blair and Proctor exchanged glances and nodded.

"Excellent," the Prince said. "My only goal tonight is to get the truth out of you two, so I can, indeed, make my little humble profit." He slowly pulled a pair of slick, black leather gloves from his breast pocket and put them on.

Proctor shrugged. He was getting tired of this. "What could we possibly tell you? I don't even know what you're talking about." Evidently, they weren't there to rob his iPad or his Rolex.

"I'm talking about the ring," the Prince said, adjusting the black gloves. "I've been informed that you are in possession of a certain ring that is very important to me and to my latest business venture. It's something I discovered a while ago and I've been pursuing it for quite some time. In fact, it's very important to many people, which is why I want it so much. You should actually be thanking me for coming here so soon. I don't think any of these other people would have been so kind to you. They have been pursuing this far longer than I have."

Proctor figured he was talking about the ring the dead guy, Rolf Braun, put on his finger right before he keeled over in the restaurant. He'd always believed it was best to tell the truth. So he shrugged and said, "I don't have the ring. I gave it to the police while they were questioning me. I didn't know that man, I didn't want his horrid ring, and it's certainly not something I'd wear out in public anywhere. There was a *buffalo* on the front."

The Prince laughed and sent his assistant, Garth, a look. Garth removed his suit jacket and threw it on the coffee table. He was wearing a see-through shirt and his entire upper body was exposed through the sheer material. His chest popped and his abs had ridges. He looked like one of those clichéd gym types Proctor saw all over Los Angeles: too many steroids, not a great face, and no brains.

"I think it's funny," the Prince said. "You're very convincing. It would be easy to believe you don't have the ring. I even wish I could believe you, because you're so pretty."

Proctor felt a rush of anger pass through his body. He hated it when someone doubted his word. He set his jaw and said, "But I *don't* have it. I told you I gave it to the police. Why the hell would I want an ugly ring like that? Do I look like the kind of person that would wear something like that vulgar buffalo?" He turned to Blair and asked, "Why doesn't he think I'm telling the truth? This is insane." He turned back to the Prince: "It's not my problem you can't tell when a good, decent person is telling the truth."

So far, Blair had been unusually silent, which wasn't like him, at least from what Proctor had seen so far. Blair glanced at Proctor, furrowed his eyebrows, and didn't say a word.

Garth reached down and adjusted his crotch. Then he pulled down his zipper and pulled a long, thick semi-erect cock out of his suit pants. When he stroked it, he smiled and looked at Proctor with a devious glance.

Proctor blinked. This was all he needed now.

The Prince said, "I'm laughing because it is funny." Then he turned to Blair and asked, "Do you know why I'm laughing so hard?"

Blair sent him a glare and said, in a deadpan voice, "Because you don't really know what the hell to think or believe right now. You're desperate right now and you're willing to do anything to get that ring back. You don't care what is or isn't true, nor do you care whom you hurt or what kind of damage or pain you cause someone else. You have no respect for human life. It's much easier for you to think he's lying so you can justify the torture you're going to put him through to get what you want, even if he doesn't have the ring."

The Prince smiled. "You're very perceptive. Torture for some is pleasure. For others, it's pain."

Proctor blinked again. "*torture*? I'm not into anything like that, dude." He tried not to look at the blond assistant's huge dick. But it was like trying not to watch an accident on the side of the road.

Blair said, "I'm sure you'll torture him until he breaks and tells you what you want to know. At least, you think that's what will happen."

"But I don't *know* anything," Proctor said. He wished Blair would shut the fuck up. He didn't want to be tortured. He didn't want that big blond assistant's dick anywhere near him.

They didn't seem to be paying attention to Proctor. The Prince gazed into Blair's eyes without blinking, and said, "You seem to understand what's going on here better than your friend."

"I've been around the block," Blair said. Garth pulled his balls out of his pants, licked his palm a few times, and started groping himself in front of everyone.

Blair grimaced and looked the other way.

"Okay," Proctor said. "He needs to put his junk away, seriously. This is getting freaky now, man." Why, if poor Jane were to walk into the living room right now and she found a big tall blond man groping his nuts and pulling his dick, she'd faint dead away. Jane was the sensible, virginal type in gum soled shoes and gingham. She was more frightened of dick than guns.

The Prince smiled and crossed to where Garth was standing. He reached down, slowly stroked his assistant's dick with the black glove, and said, "Wait until you see what goodies I have in store for you now. No spoilers, but I can tell you that it's going to be like nothing you've ever experienced before."

Proctor sent the Prince an intense stare. He had to make this guy believe him. "The problem is that I really don't have the goddamn ring. So you're wasting your fucking time."

While Garth began to remove his clothing, the Prince slowly moved toward the sofa and kneeled down in front of Proctor. He reached for Proctor's knees and slowly ran his hands up the sides of Proctor's legs. While he did this, Proctor remained silent, too terrified to speak or even gulp. The Prince's large hands in black leather stopped at Proctor's groin. He gazed down between Proctor's legs and licked his lips. Then he lifted his right hand, licked his index finger, and ran his finger slowly down the left side of Proctor's face.

As the Prince was about to reach for Proctor's cock with his other hand, Blair bolted forward, lunged at Garth, and pounced on top of him. A floor lamp fell and crashed to the floor in a million pieces. A white chair fell sideways and a potted jade plant in Proctor's favorite French cache pot tipped over. Dirt spilled all over the shiny hardwood floor. Garth was naked from the waist down now. He and Blair rolled around on the floor in the dirt as Blair tried to get the gun out of his hand. At one point, Blair shoved his knee between Garth's legs and the gun flew over the coffee table and landed about a foot away from Proctor.

Blair shouted, "Get the gun."

Without pausing to think, Proctor gave the Prince a good shove and scrambled to the floor for the gun. As he reached for it, the Prince grabbed it at the same time. They struggled with the gun for a moment, until Proctor kicked him in the nuts and crawled to the other side of the sofa on his hands and knees. He'd never held a gun; he wasn't sure what to do or how to work it. He turned and pointed the gun at the Prince, then focused on what Blair was doing. Blair was on top of Garth, with a hand on the guy's throat and the other between his legs. Proctor got a sick feeling in the pit of his stomach. Though Blair was working hard, he didn't seem like a good match for the big blond guy.

At the exact moment Garth shoved himself away from Blair, Proctor asked, "What should I do now?" His hands were shaking and the gun was still pointed at the Prince.

Blair reached for a fireplace poker and screamed, "Shoot it, goddammit." Then he swung the poker at Garth, missed him, and cracked one of Proctor's beloved antique French vases.

"Hey," Proctor said. "That's worth a small fortune. Be careful."

Blair took another swing at the blond man, demolished a small reproduction Faberge egg, and said, "Shoot the fucking gun." He seemed to be swinging without rhyme or reason. But at least he was trying.

Proctor didn't care about much about reproduction Faberge. He could always replace them. But he didn't want to lose his entire antique collection because of these two low-life thugs. "Just be careful where you swing that thing, idiot. This is my house. Focus on splitting his fucking head, not my antiques."

"Just shoot," Blair said. "Pull the fucking trigger." He was swinging faster and lower, trying to club Garth between the legs to bring him down. But he wasn't having much luck. Garth was laughing at him the entire time. He even reached down and shook his dick at one point.

Proctor stretched out his arms and tried to steady his shaking hands. The gun tipped sideways and he wasn't sure how to hold it. He felt like Jane would probably feel holding a big cock. He set his finger on the trigger, closed his eyes, and pulled it. A shot rang out and a large Japanese plate on the mantel cracked into four large pieces and fell to the hearth. But instead of worrying about the Japanese plate, Proctor felt a surge of power and energy pass through his body. This was almost as good as sex. His heart began to race and his feet tingled. He pulled the trigger again, the Prince ducked, and he clipped the bronze arm of a rock crystal sconce above the fireplace.

When Proctor almost thought they were winning, Garth lunged forward and kicked Blair in the jaw. He sent Blair flying across the living room. He landed on the sofa, flat on his back with his mouth half open. At the exact moment the assistant lunged at Blair, the Prince attacked

Proctor from the side and yanked the gun right out of his hands. Then the Prince shoved Proctor so hard Proctor landed on the other end of the sofa, head-to-head with Blair.

"Are you okay?" Blair asked Proctor. He shook his head and adjusted his jacket.

"I'm okay," he said. "How's your nose?"

"I'll live," Blair said.

The blond assistant looked down on them and laughed. He removed his sheer shirt and crossed to the sofa stark naked. He leaned over, rubbed his balls up against Proctor's face, and laughed.

Proctor closed his mouth and held his breath. Evidently, the big slob hadn't showered that day and his crotch reeked. There was nothing that could make Proctor gag more than this kind of raw, odiferous calamity.

The Prince pointed the gun at them and said, "Get up and get into the kitchen now. You want to play? Wait until you see what I have in store for you now." After all the fighting, his voice remained smooth and calm. He didn't even seem to be struggling for breath.

Blair sent him a glare. "I'll have a grilled cheese on rye." He glanced up at Garth and gestured at him with his thumb. "But hold the dill pickles and vinegar. I've had enough of that *smell* from this dude to last me a lifetime."

Chapter Six

Though Blair had been joking about the grilled cheese, Proctor was a little surprised to see that all eight burners on his stovetop were bright red. The dark-haired guy pointed the gun while naked Garth removed all their clothes and tied them both to bar stools at the center island. Garth didn't seem to care much about Blair. But while he tied Proctor up, he took every chance he could to rub his genitals against Proctor's hands. When he was finished, he reached down, shoved his hand down the back of the bar stool, and played with Proctor's ass for a minute.

Blair and Proctor exchanged glances. Blair gritted his teeth and said, "You're not going to find any rings down there, buddy. That's scared territory. No man's land."

The Prince laughed. He glanced at Proctor and said, "I don't think your friend likes it when someone puts his hand down there."

Proctor rolled his eyes. "I'm not too fond of it myself."

The blond man removed his hand from Proctor's ass and licked his index finger.

When the Prince reached into the refrigerator, he didn't pull out the ingredients for grilled cheese sandwiches. Instead, he pulled out the long, thick piece of salami and carried it back to the stovetop, dangling it back and forth as if trying to make an obscene point.

Blair glanced at Proctor and gulped. "What the hell is *that* thing doing in our refrigerator? I pegged you as the vegan/tofu California type."

Proctor shrugged. "I like a nice piece of salami once in a while. Is there a law against that?"

"Whatever makes you happy, baby," said Blair. "I prefer liverwurst and onions on rye myself."

The Prince held the salami over the hot stovetop and let it dangle.

"That thing has to be over a foot long," Blair said. "I figured you liked them big, but that's obnoxious."

54

"I buy big ones so there's always some in the house," Proctor said. Why did Blair have to turn everything into a sexual innuendo? It was nothing more than a simple piece of meat.

"I guess you do," Blair said, gaping at the salami.

The Prince's lips remained pinched. Their banter didn't seem to amuse him. He reached for a set of tongs and grabbed the salami. Then, while Blair and Proctor watched with bugged eyes, he lowered the salami onto the burning hot stovetop and watched it sizzle for a moment. When he lifted it, he turned the burnt side toward them and said, "It's fascinating to watch burning meat. I can't tell you how much of a thrill I get."

Garth smiled and rubbed his dick against Proctor's arm. He was fully erect now. His cock had one of those exaggerated curves that Proctor had never been too fond of. (The few times he'd let a guy with a curved dick fuck him, he found he had to be on his back with his legs up high, so it wouldn't hurt.) Proctor winced and turned his head. He tried not to inhale through his nose.

"I think it's time our friend started to feel a little heat now," the Prince said, lifting his voice a notch. He turned to his blond assistant. "Why don't you bring the pretty one a little closer now? You can bend him over the stove, spread his pretty legs, and stand right behind him. I'll bet he likes that. Then we can get his face a little closer to the burner."

Proctor turned to Garth and said, "Don't you touch me. I'm not going over there."

Blair's eyebrows went up. "How do you know he wasn't talking about me?" He sounded insulted.

"Because he said, 'the pretty one.' 'You're the annoying one."

The Prince lowered the salami again. It sizzled a minute longer; the skin turned black and it bubbled. He glanced at Garth and said, "Bring the pretty boy here *now*. I'm sure he'd love to know what this glorious heat is like while he has *your* nice big salami between his legs, Garth."

The blond assistant grabbed his curved erection and slapped it against Proctor's arm three times. The slaps stung and made loud cracks. Then he reached down to lift Proctor of the bar stool.

"Wait," Proctor said. "I'm not lying. I don't have the ring. I gave it to the police. I swear I did."

The Prince still didn't seem convinced. "Bring him over here. I think he needs to learn a lesson in honesty."

Garth lifted Proctor off the bar stool and held him in his arms. It couldn't have been easy. He was still tied up. But he carried him effortlessly and gently to the other side of the island and stood him up in front of the hot stovetop. He grabbed Proctor by the waist and slammed into him from behind. He shoved his erection into the trenches of Proctor's ass and started bucking his hips very slowly, preparing for the mount.

Proctor was helpless. There was only one thing he could do. "I'm telling you the truth. I'm pleading with you. I don't have the ring. I gave it to the police. What do you want me to do? Make something up and send you looking for something I don't have? Should I lie?"

Garth grunted and spread his legs. He leaned back, pointed the head of his cock toward Proctor's opening, and squeezed Proctor's hips. He spit on his erection, which sent a chill down Proctor's spine. He was about to enter Proctor without a condom or lube when the Prince dropped the salami in the kitchen sink and switched off the stovetop.

He lifted his arm and waved, signaling Garth to stop. The blond man stood up and carried Proctor back to the bar stool. When Proctor was seated, Garth kissed him on the cheek and ran his thick warm tongue along the side of his face.

Then Prince crossed to them and glared at Proctor. He said, "Okay, you claim the ring is with the police. It won't be difficult to check that out. I have more than a few connections there." He crossed to where Garth was standing and reached down for his erection. He wrapped his hand around the curved cock and said, "You can be sure I'll check it out. And if I don't find my ring there, you can be sure I'll be back. And this time I won't be so kind." Then he yanked Garth's dick and pulled him into the living room.

* * *

When the front door slammed with a loud thud and the Prince and his unwashed assistant were gone, Proctor slid his barstool sideways, with care so he wouldn't topple over. He wanted to be back-to-back with Blair.

"What are you doing now?" Blair asked.

"I'm trying to get behind you so I can untie you, and then you can untie me, genius. Then we can both get dressed and you can leave me alone for good."

When he was up against the back of Blair's barstool, he fumbled with the ties around Blair's wrists for a few minutes. It wasn't easy. He couldn't seem to get a tight enough grip on the ties to unknot them. But he eventually loosened something, and a minute later Blair shook his wrists free and stood up.

Blair removed the ties from his naked body and scratched his balls. Then he crossed to the stovetop to turn the burners off.

"Hey," Proctor said. "What the fuck are you doing? You're supposed to untie me first, not turn off the burners." He'd jerked the barstool around again. He was facing the center island, watching every move Blair made. Though he'd already had sex with Blair twice, this was the first time he'd had a chance to see his naked body. Blair wasn't a muscle-bound god like the smelly blond guy. He had a nice, thin defined body, and the muscles he did have were pronounced and cut. His legs were even, not bowed or knock-kneed, with those cute little indentations just above his knee where his thigh muscles began. He had a little hair on his chest, and a little more on his legs. Evidently, he trimmed his pubic hair slightly with an electric razor, but he didn't shave it all off. His dick wasn't too big or too small. He didn't seem self-conscious in the least about being naked in front of Proctor. In fact, he could have been showing off. Proctor couldn't help noticing he had a semi-erection swinging back and forth, and he made no attempt to hide it.

Blair switched off the last burner and said, "Safety first, baby," in a cocky tone. Then he crossed to the other side of the counter and stood in front of Proctor with a huge grin and a slightly bigger dick. His semi-erection was turning into a full erection, and from the way he was smiling, he seemed way too proud of it.

Proctor rolled his eyes. He gaped at Blair's dick and said, "Put that thing away and untie me, idiot. You and your dick are going home and I want to go to bed." He decided to forego the salami that night. After what the Prince had done to the salami, he'd lost his appetite.

"I'm not going to untie you just yet," Blair said. He now had a smug, lighthearted expression, as if he knew he had all the power and he was enjoying it.

Proctor felt his face grow warm and he bit his bottom lip. "Listen, you'd better untie me right now if you know what's good for you. I don't want to talk about keeping the agency open. I don't want to talk any more about how you can turn it into a money-making business. You'll only be wasting your time."

Blair scratched his balls again and his erection jumped. "That's not what I want to talk about." He glanced down, pointed to his dick, and said, "You be good now." He looked up again and said, "He has a mind of his own sometimes."

Proctor smiled. Blair could be an idiot, but he had a sense of humor. In a low tone, Proctor said, "I'm not having sex again with you, so get that out of your head right now." He gestured with his head at Blair's dick. "Tell *him* that, too."

"That's not it either. This isn't about dick, even though I know how much you like it." He bucked his hips a few times and slapped his thighs.

Proctor groaned out loud. "Then what is it? I'm tired. I want to go to bed. It's all over now and the bad guys are gone."

Blair shrugged. "You're going to have to come with me. You can't stay here tonight, because it's not over yet."

"Why not?" He had a bad feeling and he sent Blair a glare. "*What did you do?*"

"I have the ring. When you handed me the ring to give to the police, I switched the ring with one I was wearing. It was a graduation gift from my Uncle Sonny, black onyx with my initial in gold set in the center. I never really liked that ring much. I never really liked Uncle Sonny much either, but I digress."

Procter clenched his fists and jerked the barstool forward. He glared at Blair and said, "You're telling me that you have the ring and that I almost wound up getting fucked by a moron with a dick like a boomerang, then burned in the face? You could have given them the ring and all this would have been over long ago? You fucking asshole. Do you know what you put me through? You only did this to keep the agency going. I should have known better."

"You're a loon," Blair said in a dejected voice. "If you think I want to work with *you* now, you're flattering yourself. All I was interested in was your celebrity, not you personally. The last thing I want is some prissy, aging circuit queen in tight pants latching onto me."

Proctor's eyebrow's pointed down. He glared at Blair and said, almost in a growl, "Prissy, aging circuit queen in tight pants? Latching on to *you*? You're calling *me* a prissy circuit queen after the way you fought back there in the living room?"

Blair gestured with his hands and his erection jumped again. "Calm down, baby. It's all good. I protected you. I fought them off for you."

"Ha," Proctor said. "You fought like a fucking sissy boy, A *pussy*. That's why I'm tied up right now. If you knew how to throw a decent punch, none of this would have happened."

Blair's jaw dropped. He pouted. "Ha. You're calling *me* a pussy? I thought I fought pretty good back there. That guy was three times my size."

"My assistant, Jane, could have kicked his ass better," Proctor said. He didn't really mean it. He'd been surprised at how well Blair could fight in a situation like that. On the surface, Blair looked a lot like one of those handsome professional golfers who never get their hands dirty or a preppie young Republican on his way to a tea party rally. But the way he'd lunged after the blond guy had, indeed, been impressive. Only Proctor didn't want him to know this. He was still too angry about being called a prissy aging circuit queen to be nice.

"Just calm down," Blair said. "I know you don't mean that."

"Don't tell me to calm down, idiot," Proctor said. "Those thugs are going to find out the police have the wrong ring and they are going to come after me. You heard them."

"That's why I have to take you with me tonight," Blair said.

"I wouldn't go anywhere with you," Proctor said. "You must be joking."

"You're not going to move from that spot unless I untie you," Blair said. "And there's no way I'm going to untie you unless I know for a fact that you are centered, relaxed, and thinking clearly. I've never met a more emotional dude in my life. Dude, get a grip."

Proctor gritted his teeth. "I am completely relaxed. Untie me, asshole."

Blair smiled and took a step closer. "You don't look relaxed. The vein in your neck is still popping. I think there's only one thing that will relax you. From my limited personal experience with you in these matters, this seems to be the only thing that will do the trick." He reached down, grabbed his dick, and took two more steps toward Proctor. He shook his dick a few times, then hopped up on the counter. When he was seated on the beige granite, he pulled Proctor's barstool closer and spread his legs.

Blair's dick was only inches from Proctor's lips. Proctor turned his head to the left and said, "Untie me right now. Get down off that counter and let me go. We're not going to fuck again, not tonight or ever."

"Not until you're more relaxed and I know I can trust you to come anywhere with me."

Proctor took a quick breath, trying not to inhale the tweedy, musky aroma coming from between Blair's sexy legs. Unlike the despicable blond muscle guy, the smell coming from between Blair's legs was appealing enough to cause a stir between Proctor's legs. Blair didn't smell like perfume, but he wasn't repulsive either. His neatly trimmed crotch smelled the way a man should smell in a good way, not an offensive way. "Okay, I'm relaxed. Close your legs and untie me."

Blair rubbed Proctor's cheek with the head of his dick and smiled. "I don't think so," he said. "I think you need something first, just to make sure you're relaxed."

Proctor rolled his eyes. "I don't need anything." He glanced at Blair's dick. "Especially not that thing."

Blair laughed. He moved even closer and rubbed the entire shaft along the side of Proctor's face very gently.

Proctor drew another quick breath. He was about to repeat that he was relaxed. He was about to beg to be untied if that was what it took to get free. But when he inhaled this time, and he took in the sweet, musky smell of Blair, he opened his mouth instead. Then he closed his eyes and started sucking on the head of Blair's dick very slowly. He wrapped his lips around it gently and slid them back and forth. He'd sucked his fair share of guys off in his lifetime, but this time it seemed to be different. It tasted better and felt better than before. All he had to do was touch it gently and he felt something warm and comfortable pass through his entire body, a surge or emotion he couldn't explain. If this had been the first dick he'd ever sucked in his life, he would have been ruined forever because nothing would have been able to compare with it.

While he sucked gently on the head, Blair spread his legs wider and reached for the sides of Proctor's head. Blair caressed his head with subtle strokes, then moaned softly and whispered, "Ah baby, you are so good at this. You're so damn pretty. I can't even imagine what it's like to be as pretty as you are."

A few minutes later, Proctor's head went forward and he slowly sucked Blair's erection all the way into his mouth. He forgot all about being tied up. The only thing he cared about was the cock inside his mouth. He moved slowly, with precision. He kept his tongue flat against the bottom of the shaft and his cheeks indented slightly from the mild suction. Proctor liked to work his way up to intense sucking with caution. He knew how to build tension in order to create unforgettable explosions.

From the first day he'd started, he'd been a natural cocksucker. He seemed to know, partly from his own feelings as a man, how to make another man truly happy this way. It was the rare man he couldn't get off by just using his lips and tongue alone.

As the suction grew more intense and Proctor's head began to move back and forth, Blair threw his naked legs over the back of the barstool and he held Proctor's shoulders for support. In this distorted position, he moaned and begged for more in deep, slow whispers. He pleaded with Proctor to keep sucking faster. At one point, when Proctor opened his eyes for a second to see what Blair was doing, Blair's head was tilted back and his mouth opened wider.

When Proctor finally tasted Blair's pre-come, he tightened his jaw and pressed his tongue against the bottom of Blair's shaft with more intensity. His pre-come tasted sweeter than most guys', and the head of his cock seemed to swell more, too. Proctor knew he was ready to come. He maintained even suction, never missing a beat, while Blair's body went rigid. Though Proctor was erect, he *couldn't* touch himself and he didn't care. He enjoyed satisfying Blair this way. He didn't need to come every time he did this. He felt a thrill between his legs, which cased his balls to tighten, knowing he had the power to do this to Blair.

A few minutes after the pre-come started, Blair dug his fingers into Proctor's shoulder, let out a loud grunt from the bottom of his diaphragm, and sent a load of come down the back of Proctor's throat. Proctor continued to suck. He didn't gag or choke or wince.

After that, while Proctor was still sucking the last drops out of him, Blair relaxed his muscles and said, "I'm so sorry I did that, buddy." He caressed the top of Proctor's head. "I'm so sorry I didn't ask if it was okay to come first. I'm a huge shithead. I'm a selfish fucker. It's just that I couldn't help it. I don't know what you were doing down there, but I've never had anyone do anything like that before. It's like my dick was caught in a freaking wind tunnel."

Proctor almost laughed at Blair's reaction. It sounded too silly to comprehend at that late hour. This was the exact quality he couldn't figure out in Blair: he was serious and competent, yet silly and idiotic at the same time. So Proctor took one last suck and slid his head back. Blair's dick slipped out of his mouth and he said, "Stop apologizing. I knew what I was doing. If I didn't want to do it, I wouldn't have done it."

Proctor shrugged. "You were with an amateur," he said. "And

there's nothing wrong with the taste of come. In fact, yours is actually sweeter than most guys I've blown. I always figure that if I'm going to suck a dick, I might as well finish the job like a real man. Otherwise, why bother?" Then he leaned forward, sucked Blair back into his mouth, and held him there until he went flaccid. Those last few drops were always the sweetest.

* * *

After Blair untied Proctor, Blair got dressed and Proctor went up to his bedroom to pack a small bag. He wasn't sure how long he'd be gone; he packed as if he were going away for a long weekend. By the time he was dressed in jeans and a white shirt, he met Blair at the front door. Only Blair wasn't standing there waiting patiently. He was on top of the hall table looking down at Constance.

"What are you doing up there?" Proctor asked.

"You might not know this, but there's a leopard in your house," Blair said.

Proctor bent down and kissed Constance on top of the head. Then he looked up at Blair and said, "She's just a big Bengal cat, not a leopard, you fool. She's a little larger than most. But any idiot can see she's as harmless as a fluffy little kitten. Aren't you, baby? Is that big mean man scaring you?" He always talked to Constance in a baby talk voice. He liked to hear her purr.

Blair rubbed his jaw and glanced down at Constance. She was glaring at him. The tip of her tail was curling back and forth, which was a sure sign she was pissed off about something. "She wasn't harmless with *me*. She hissed, swiped her claws, and chased me up here." He tried to lower his leg and Constance hissed at him again. "See what I mean? That's a wildcat. And she looks hungry."

Proctor set his bag down and hugged Constance. He kissed her again and said, "That's my little baby girl." While Constance licked his hand, he looked up at Blair. "I've never seen her react this way. She's the most passive, lazy cat I've ever met. That's why you didn't see her around when those thugs were here. She was probably hiding somewhere. She hides most of the time. She must not trust you for some reason."

"The feeling is mutual," Blair said.

Proctor picked Constance up and carried her into the kitchen so Blair could climb down from the hall table and pull himself together. He fed her, left a note for Jane letting her know he'd be gone for a few days, and to book a flight to New York first thing the next morning. He also asked Jane to bring Constance to the vet, where Proctor always boarded her when he traveled. Jane lived in a small guest house on the property. He didn't want her around the house in case the thugs came back looking for him. And he couldn't leave Constance in an empty house. He didn't trust the thugs and he knew they were capable of doing anything. He figured he'd send Jane on a wild goose chase to New York. He told her in the note he wanted her to spend a week there looking at apartments because he was thinking of moving to New York full time. In the morning, he would call her and make sure she went fast. He would insist. He knew Jane well. She would love the trip to New York, and Jane would do anything he asked her to do. Thankfully, he still had good credit and a little money left from the businesses he'd liquidated. She could use his credit card for expenses.

By the time he met Blair outside, Blair was sitting behind the wheel in the BMW and Proctor climbed into the passenger seat without saying a word. He didn't feel like driving, and Blair seemed like the type who liked that kind of control. Proctor was too tired to argue. He wasn't even sure where they were going. He figured he'd find out soon enough.

When they reached Wilshire Boulevard, the silence was so pronounced Proctor was afraid to cough or clear his throat. Blair must have felt the same way, because he started a conversation that was nothing more than small talk. "I'll bet you love all those romantic movies on TV on the women's channels," he said.

Proctor sent him a snide glance and said, "Not all. Just some of them. I really love the old Neil Simon movies from the 1970s. I cry every time I see *Only When I Laugh*. Those movies made during that period, when Neil Simon was married to Marsha Mason, are classics now. I once went to a charity event I didn't want to attend, just to stand in line and meet Marsha Mason in person. When she recognized *me* from *my* poster, I almost dropped dead on the spot."

Blair hit the gas and passed a slower car. He twirled his finger and laughed. "Sounds fascinating. I'm sorry I wasn't there, too."

"I'll bet you like those action adventure films," Proctor said. He could just see Blair now, sitting in front of the TV, with a beer in one hand and a bowl of popcorn in the other, scratching his balls and watching something where people were being shot or blown into a million pieces.

Blair smiled without taking his eyes off the road. "I like some of them. I once stood in line for a day to meet Arnold Schwarzenegger. I've seen every *Terminator* film ever made at least four times."

Proctor sighed and glanced at the buildings passing them by. "Why am I not surprised?"

They rode the rest of the way in relative silence, until they reached a familiar building and Blair turned right into the parking lot. It took a moment for Proctor to recognize the building because it was late and he didn't go there often. It was the building where the offices for the detective agency and Proctor's dentist were located.

They parked in an assigned space that had Blair's name in front of it. Then they went into a back door of the building that Blair said most people didn't know about. He was the kind of guy who knew shortcuts and back doors well. If there was an angle or a hook, he'd figure it out. On the way to the office, Blair took the security guard aside and said something to him Proctor didn't hear. When Blair returned, he said, "I told security to be on the lookout. They owe me a few favors. We'll be safe here. These guys are the best." Then he set his palm on the small of Proctor's back and led him up to the office.

When they stepped into Blair's office, Proctor set his Gucci bag down and turned to face Blair. "I guess this is home, sweet home, for a while."

"It's the safest place right now," Blair said. He seemed more serious now. He wasn't joking, or talking too much. He opened a closet door and pulled out a puffy black blanket and a white pillow. He held them up and said, "I've spent a few nights here before. I like to be prepared."

Proctor turned and smiled at him. He didn't say anything.

"Why are you giving me the bad boy look?" Blair asked. "What did I do now to piss you off?"

"It's not that," Proctor said. It was late, too late to argue. "You didn't do anything. I'm just a little shocked you didn't take me to some sleazy motel and try to get me in bed in some tacky room with bad sheets, 24-hour porn, and a vibrating bed."

Blair smiled. He set the cover and pillow on a desk and crossed to where Proctor was standing. "After what happened in the kitchen back at your place, I think we've gone beyond that point. You can enjoy sucking my dick right here, where it won't cost a dime, as well as anywhere else." Then he turned, picked up the bed things, and carried them to a long, brown leather sofa against the back wall.

Proctor watched Blair spread out the cover and fluff the pillow. "It probably won't happen again."

Blair glanced back and said, "Is there someone who should know you're not going to be home?"

"I left a note for my assistant, Jane, in the kitchen when I fed Constance," Proctor said. "I didn't go into details. I just said I'd be gone, for her to take Constance to the vet, and for her to book a flight to New York in the morning to go look for apartments. I figured she shouldn't be in the house either. I'll call her early in the morning to make sure she listens. I'm sure those crooks won't be back during the daytime."

Blair smiled. "You're already thinking like a good detective. But I was talking about someone special, like a boyfriend or family."

Proctor took a deep breath and exhaled. "I don't have much family, just an aunt back east. There's no boyfriend. In fact, I'm not sure I've ever referred to any of the men I've been with as boyfriends." Then he smiled and said. "I want to thank you for what you did back at my place, when you went after those guys. No one has ever done anything like that for me before. You weren't very good at it. But you can't help it if you're not a fighter."

Blair fluffed the pillow again. His voice went up with a lilt. "I see you're still in a nasty mood."

"I'm not in a nasty mood," Proctor said. "I just want to know what's happening. I want to know if you have an overview of all this and you know where it's all going. Someone has to be in charge, and I don't know what the hell I'm doing. Most of all, I'm exhausted and scared to death."

Blair stood up and said, "You should turn in now. You need sleep."

Proctor sent him a confused look. "You don't know what you're doing, not a clue."

"Are you saying I'm not a competent detective?"

"I'm not saying that," Proctor said. "I'm just looking for answers. When I make decisions, I like to make them based on sound information that's given to me. So far, I'm not getting anything from you."

When he said this, in such a low, defeated tone, Blair walked up to him and caressed his cheek very gently. Blair seemed to sense his fear and want to make it right. "You're going to have to trust me. There's no one better than me." Then he turned and headed to the door.

When he reached the door, he stopped and hesitated for a moment. He smiled and sent Proctor a sideways glance. "I'll be in the conference room if you need anything, unless you'd like me stay in here with you. We can get naked and I can climb on top of you and keep you warm."

"I'd rather sleep alone," Proctor said. Having sex with Blair had probably been a huge mistake. The last thing he needed or wanted was to actually start sleeping with him on a regular basis. They were too different people from two different worlds; they would always wind up fighting. And as soon as this business with the ring was settled, Proctor would close the agency and go back to his real life. Maybe he would move to New York to work on his modeling career.

Chapter Seven

When Proctor tried to turn over on his back the next morning, his legs were pinned to the leather sofa and he couldn't move. He'd fallen asleep face down the night before. His left arm hung over the sofa and his right was stuck between his chest and the leather. At first, he thought he was having a nightmare. He felt disconnected and separated from reality. He wasn't sure where he was or how he'd arrived there. Then he felt a wisp of warm breath on his neck and it all came rushing back to him: the hideous blind date with the dentist, the dead guy named Rolf Braun, the police station, the Prince and blond smelly Garth, and winding up in the detective agency with Blair Huntingdon.

He opened his eyes and turned his head sideways. As he glanced up, Blair Huntingdon opened his eyes and smiled down on him. Blair kissed him on the lips and said, "Good morning, baby."

Proctor closed his eyes and groaned. "What are you doing in here on top of me? I thought you were sleeping in the conference room."

Blair's right arm went down and he ran his palm up and down the side of Proctor's ass. "It got lonely in the conference room. I figured I'd come in here and keep you company."

"So you took off all your clothes and climbed on top of me," Proctor said.

"Don't worry," Blair said. "I took off your clothes, too. You didn't seem to mind."

Proctor had a vague memory of him coming in and removing his clothes. Proctor had been too exhausted to fight him. Besides, he was also a little afraid to sleep alone after what had happened with the thugs. But he didn't want Blair to know he remembered, or that he felt safer with Blair there. "You took off my clothes while I was sleeping? What are you, some kind of a gay creep?"

He felt Blair's dick pressing into his ass. "I was probably sound asleep. And stop poking me with your dick right now. Anyone could walk in here on us. I swear, you're always horny."

"I locked the door. I'm the only one with a key. Besides, it's too early."

Though he didn't like the way Blair had talked him into getting naked while he was half asleep, he couldn't deny that he did like the way Blair was rubbing up against him now. Blair's lips felt soft on his neck, and his light stubble sent shocks in waves up his spine. He wondered how a man who could annoy him so much could also make every single nerve ending in his body feel such pleasure. "I told you we weren't going to do this anymore. So get off of me and put your dick away." Proctor also knew the more he refused, the more Blair would beg. His type was always that way.

"But I'm so hard, baby. What am I supposed to do with it?"

"You can jack off in the shower, for all I care."

Blair wrapped his arms around Proctor and squeezed him. He continued bucking his hips. He licked Proctor's ear and said, "Just one more time and we'll never do this again. I swear on my life."

Proctor's voice grew weaker. His own erection was pressing into the leather and Blair was still licking his ear. He had to be strong. This was a mistake. "No," he said. "We're not doing this again."

"You don't sound very convincing," Blair said. He bit his earlobe gently. "I think you want me to beg you. I think you know exactly what you're doing. I don't mind. I'm not too proud to beg for tail."

"*Tail?*"

"You know what I mean. I don't mind begging."

Proctor rested his cheek on Blair's strong forearm and inhaled his aroma. He rubbed his lips against Blair's skin and said, "I don't want you to beg. I'm not like that. I'm not one of those bottom guys who like to tease and play games."

"Then let me fuck you one more time," Blair said. "There's a condom on the coffee table. I brought it in with me last night just in case."

Proctor gently bit his arm. "Yeah, just in case. You knew exactly what you were doing."

Blair removed his arms from Proctor's body, but he didn't get up off the sofa. His lower body remained in position, as if he couldn't wait to start grinding again. He yanked off the black comforter and reached for the condom on the coffee table. He covered his dick with the lubed condom so fast that Proctor barely had time to open his legs. Then he turned slightly, guided the head into Proctor's hole, and slid all the way to the bottom with one profound plunge.

Proctor's toes curled. He closed his eyes and gasped for breath. There was no pain with Blair, just a quick moment of discomfort that came in a flash and disappeared. After that, Proctor's body took Blair as if he were the last missing piece to a very complicated puzzle. While Blair whispered about how tight and soft Proctor's hole was, Proctor reached for Blair's hand and started sucking his fingers.

Blair didn't object. He started moving faster and said, "Yeah, baby, suck. You look so fucking hot doing that. Damn, you have sweet lips."

This time Blair didn't slide all the way in and out like he'd done in the parking garage and the elevator. He fucked deep and hard, only sliding halfway in and out. He moved his pelvis and the rest of his body remained stationary. Proctor continued to suck Blair's fingers, gasping for breath every so often, moaning softly each time Blair went deeper. In this position, Blair's dick stimulated his prostate in a constant way, and his own dick rubbed against the soft leather. When his left leg fell off the sofa, Blair started pounding so fast, the sofa slid down toward the window. The arm of the sofa hit a side table. The side table jerked and a tall black lamp tipped sideways and hit the floor. This was the first time Proctor had ever been with a man who didn't slow down or take a break. Blair didn't change positions, and he didn't lose a beat of momentum.

A moment before they came, Blair started grunting. Proctor imagined they'd been fucking for over a half hour, at least. Proctor's entire body was drenched in perspiration by then. His back was covered with Blair's perspiration and Blair's sweet smell. He knew Blair was close when Blair's chest began to heave and the fingers in his mouth tightened. Blair started fucking so fast Proctor heard the loud slaps against his ass. He felt Blair's balls banging into the bottom of his ass.

"I'm there, baby," Blair said. "I'm riding the line."

Proctor didn't speak. He sucked harder on Blair's fingers and nodded. He'd always preferred it when men came this way

A second after that, they both went over the edge together. If Proctor has been asked to describe it, the only way he could have done it was to refer to an arc: the climax began in silence, built upward in gradual intervals, peaked at the top, and slowly tapered off until there was nothing left but pleasant sensations and remnants of two people expressing something more powerful than Proctor could describe at the time. At the peak, Blair's upper body curled back and he moaned the word "fuck" out loud—long and slow, in a wrecked, disconnected stage whisper. Blair's climax came from deep inside his body, traveled in every direction, and finished with an outrageous ejaculation on the sofa cushion beneath him.

While Blair remained deep inside, as he regained his senses, Proctor relaxed every muscle and went limp beneath him. And when Blair finally started bucking his hips again, he sent subtle shocks of pleasure to every single nerve ending in Proctor's body.

When Blair finally collapsed on top of him, he wrapped his arms around Proctor's shoulders and kissed him on the lips. "We're both soaked. I think that was pretty damn good, if I say so myself." He was still inside him, still grinding his hips.

Though Proctor had never experienced anything quite like this with another man, he didn't want Blair to know that he'd been blown away. It was the kind of sexual expression Proctor had only dreamed he would one day experience, never actually believing he would. "It wasn't bad."

Blair's head went up. He reached around and slapped Proctor on the ass so hard it tingled. "Wasn't bad? Are you serious? Baby, what we just did rocked the fucking world and you know it. Lamps flew off tables."

"Okay, it was better than usual," Proctor said. He couldn't seem to get away with anything anymore. It was as if Blair could read his mind. "Now get off me so I can take a shower and get dressed."

Blair bit his neck. "Oh, no. I'm not letting you up until you admit this was the best sex you've ever had."

Proctor smiled. Though it *was* the best sex he'd ever had, he decided to sound as if he were just saying this to placate Blair. "Okay, it was the best sex ever. You're the hottest stud ever. You have the dick of death and I'm nothing but your slave from now until the end of time. Is that better? Is that the kind of stupid shit you wanted to hear?"

"Well, that's not bad for a start."

There was only one way to end this. Proctor sighed and said, "How's this? You are the best fuck I've ever had or ever will have. No man on this Earth will ever compare to you, not now, not in the future, or in the past. You are the ultimate sex machine: a walking dick."

Blair kissed him on the cheek and pulled out fast. "That's much better. Now I'll let you up." He slapped his ass and climbed off his back.

Proctor glanced at the condom on his dick. The tip was loaded, which was a sight that gave him personal, though silent, satisfaction. He smiled and reached for Blair's hand. "Help me up now. I've been in that position for so long I'm not sure I can move."

Blair helped him to his feet and said, "We should just shower together. Why waste water? Think about the environment."

Proctor turned and headed to the bathroom door, knowing Blair was gaping at his ass the entire time. Without looking back, he said, "I prefer to shower alone. I won't be long." Then he grabbed his overnight bag, went into the bathroom, and locked the door behind him.

He didn't want Blair to see the way he was smiling.

* * *

Before anyone arrived at the office, Blair and Proctor went downtown for breakfast. Blair wolfed down eggs, bacon, pancakes, a banana, and a blueberry muffin. Proctor sat and watched him, sipping on black coffee, wearing dark glasses because he was worried there were dark circles beneath his eyes. At one point, when Blair sopped up egg yolk with a forkful of pancakes, he turned and covered his mouth. Blair smiled with egg dripping down his chin and said, "Want some? It's good."

Though Proctor hadn't eaten much the day before, he'd never been able to stand the sight of food early in the morning. Even orange juice could twist his stomach sideways and make him nauseous. He returned a smug smile and said, "No, thank you. I'm fine. But be a good boy and don't talk with your mouth full."

When they left the coffee shop, they ventured a few doors down. Proctor had no idea where they were going. "I hope you know what you're doing. This doesn't look like a place where I'd normally shop." He'd already phoned Jane after he'd showered. She assured him she would pack fast, take Constance to the vet, and head to the airport as soon as she hung up. Proctor made it sound crucial that she leave right away and not waste a moment. Jane said she would and that she'd call him from the airport in a little while to let him know what time she was departing for New York. He'd never felt so relieved to hear anyone's voice. He'd been worried the thugs would return and harm Jane.

"We have to find out why this ring is so important to those assholes," Blair said. He stopped in front of a shop and turned to face Proctor. "There must be some reason why they want it so badly."

"How are we going to do that?" Proctor asked. He was still hoping to see a sign of empowerment in Blair, and to discover they had a plan to follow.

Blair gestured to a sign above their heads that read, *Levine Fine Jewelry*. "We're going to ask a jeweler to look at the ring. Maybe it's some priceless ancient treasure."

The jeweler turned out to be an older man who stood about five feet tall. He had thin silver hair, the slim body of a young boy, and walked with a slight hunch. The jeweler glanced at the ring for a minute without saying a word. Then he pulled a loupe out of his pocket and held the ring under a bright light. He examined every angle with a deep frown. When he finally looked up, he said, "It's not even gold."

Proctor felt a pull deep in his stomach. This wasn't going well and it only confirmed what he already suspected.

Blair asked, "How much is it worth?"

"I wouldn't give you $10 bucks for it. Sorry," said the jeweler.

"But there has to be some value," Proctor said. He was hoping maybe it was some kind of famous costume jewelry design. He'd seen pieces of famous costume jewelry at auctions and knew there was a market for collectors.

The jeweler shrugged and said, "Maybe there's sentimental value. There's a tiny engraving underneath. Looks like a bunch of numbers. I can't make any sense out of it." He turned the ring over and Proctor saw small print that looked like some kind of code.

"Are you sure that isn't a manufacturer's number?" Proctor asked.

The jeweler shook his head. "I'm sure. This was definitely engraved at one point, but it looks like gibberish to me."

While they were speaking, an older man walked into the shop. He had a paunch, a bald head, and a salt and pepper mustache. He looked familiar to Proctor, but he couldn't quite place him. By that time, Blair had taken the ring out of the jeweler's hand, put it back in his pocket, and he was walking toward the exit.

Proctor thanked the jeweler and turned to leave. When he caught up with Blair outside, he pulled his arm and said, "I think that was very rude. You just left that poor man standing there in the middle of a conversation. I can't imagine what he thinks of us."

Blair set his palm on the small of Proctor's back and guided him to the passenger side of the BMW parked on the street. He opened the door for Proctor and said, "I wanted to get out of there. The guy who came in looked strange. They could be following us right now."

Proctor gulped and looked back and forth. He didn't see anyone following them, but now that Blair had said it, his heart started to race. He climbed into the car and shut his door fast, without saying another word. He didn't take a deep breath again until they were out on the street, about four blocks away from the jewelry store.

By that time Blair was singing along with something on the radio. It was an older song and Proctor couldn't remember the name. His heart rate had returned to normal and now he was clenching his fists and biting the inside of his mouth. When Blair asked him if the music bothered him, he turned his head in the opposite direction and refused to answer.

"Okay, I see we are not on speaking terms," Blair said. "I'm sorry. I wasn't informed, once again. I'd just like to know what crawled up your sweet little ass between the time we left the jewelry store and right now, because I don't think I said anything that would offend you, Your Royal Highness."

This time Proctor refused to speak to him. He wouldn't even turn and look in his direction.

Blair took a deep breath and exhaled. He slowed down for an older woman crossing the street and said, "There's nothing simple about mysteries. You don't just get the answers immediately because you want them. This isn't the modeling business. You don't just snap your fingers and everyone comes running. So the ring isn't real gold. So what?"

Proctor turned his head fast. "It's a piece of *shit*."

"Yes, it's a piece of shit," Blair said. His tone remained calm and reassuring. "But that ring definitely means something to someone. It could have something to do with the engraving on the bottom. That's what we have to figure out."

Proctor's eyebrows went up. He flung Blair a pathetic glance and said, "And you're going to figure this out? *You*, the clown? I fired you and you laughed in my face. You take me to some old jeweler who could be somebody's grandfather and knows nothing that can help us. You belch without covering your mouth while egg drips down our chin. You drive too damn fast. And I'm supposed to believe you're going to figure all this out?"

"Are you going to sit there and rant all day like a spoiled child, or do I have to shove my dick back into your mouth to shut you up?"

Proctor felt a wave of deep anger pass through his body this time. He turned and clamped his lips together. But he was too frustrated to remain silent, so he glared at Blair again and said, "Yes, I'm going rant all day, and all night, too. I'd like to know how someone who doesn't have any business experience, doesn't have any knowledge about the criminal justice system, and doesn't know a flying fuck about fighting or basic self-defense could wind up as head of a private detective agency. I've never met anyone more inept in my life."

A hurt, dejected expression formed on Blair's face. He didn't fight back this time. There were no quips or sarcastic remarks. He slowed down, pulled to the corner and lowered the passenger window.

"Why are we stopping?" Proctor said. He softened his voice. He felt a little guilty about exploding that way, but he was used to getting what he wanted whenever he wanted it. This was the first time in more years than he could remember when there weren't people groveling at his feet.

"Go get a morning paper," Blair said.

"Are you going to pull away and leave me here alone?" Proctor said. After all he'd just said, he wouldn't have blamed Blair.

"Just get the damn paper," Blair said. "I'm not going anywhere."

So Proctor climbed out of the car and went into a small grocery store. When Proctor returned with the paper, Blair told him to open to the obituary page. "What should I look for?" Proctor asked.

"Find out if someone named Dwayne Calvin died recently," Blair said. "I remember overhearing his name in the police station last night. They said he was hit by a car recently and the only witness to his death was the creep who put the ring on your finger and dropped dead in front of us at the restaurant, the one and only Mr. Rolf Braun." Blair's eyes remained focused on the road and his voice low and even. He wouldn't look Proctor in the eye.

Proctor unfolded the paper and turned to the obituary page. He glanced up and down and saw nothing. "Sorry, no Dwayne Calvin here. Any more bright ideas, Lieutenant?" It had been so long since Proctor had read a print newspaper it felt awkward in his hands. He usually got all his information on the Internet.

Blair rubbed his jaw and thought for a moment. Then he said, "Take out your iPhone and look it up on the Internet. Maybe they published it earlier."

"This is a waste of time," Proctor said. "I don't see the point of looking up some dead guy."

"Just do what I say. There has to be a connection between this Dwayne Calvin guy and Rolf Braun."

Proctor exhaled and pulled his phone out of his pocket. He went to the Internet, did a search for the morning newspaper, then did another search for the obituary of Dwayne Calvin. He almost fell sideways when the name came up. "It's here," he said. "It says Dwayne Calvin was a hang glider, a professional pilot, a part time singer, and an avid runner. He worked part time for some insurance building downtown. It also says he was struck by a car and killed instantly. Do you think this has something to do with the ring and why they're after us?" He turned off his phone and slowly turned to face Blair. "This sounds like there's a plan now. This can't be a coincidence." For the first time in a while, he felt hopeful.

Blair's eyes remained focused on the road. He tilted his head and clenched the steering wheel. "No way, dude. It can't be a plan, because I'm not capable of coming up with a plan. I'm just a monkey who peels bananas with his big feet and lets egg drip down his chin. I'm a poor businessman who has no experience in criminal justice and fights like a sissy boy. Oh yeah, that's me, the original loser who can't run a detective agency and couldn't solve a case if his life depended on it. I'm not good for anything more than a good fuck and kick in the ass. In fact, I'm such a lowlife, pathetic piece of shit I can't even piss and whistle at the same time. That's me: big, dumb Blair who has to take off his shoes and socks and pull down his zipper to count to 21. There's no way I could ever come up with a viable plan to solve this case or any other."

Proctor had highly underestimated Blair this time and now he was sorry for what he'd said. He felt so bad his eyes started to sting. He turned slowly in Blair's direction and reached for his hand. Just touching his hand sent a thrill up his legs. He squeezed his hand and said, "I'm sorry for all those things I said. I didn't mean it. I was freaking out."

"You meant every word." Blair was pouting now, and the way his bottom lip protruded looked so cute Proctor had to control himself from leaning over and kissing him while he was driving. "I could be wrong about all this and Dwayne Calvin and Rolf Braun might not even be connected. Rolf Braun could have been there when Calvin died by sheer coincidence. You might be right about me after all. Maybe I am just a big, dumb loser with egg dripping down his chin."

When Blair spoke like this, it took all the control Proctor had not to start crying right there in the car. He wished he hadn't said the things he'd said. He wished he hadn't ranted on so irrationally and hurt Blair's feelings. He squeezed his hand again and leaned forward to kiss Blair's knuckles. In a soft voice, he said, "No, you're not. You're a strong, smart, brave man. And I know you'll figure this out."

Chapter Eight

After they found out about the odd connection between Rolf Braun and Dwayne Calvin, they went to the funeral home that handled Dwayne's service. The funeral director told them Dwayne didn't have any family left and the person who had made all of Dwayne's funeral arrangements was a young man Dwayne had been dating for a while. The funeral director told them the young man's name was Selvyn Markowitz. He worked as a male stripper, and was still living in the same rented condo he'd been sharing off and on with Dwayne Calvin. At least, that was the address Selvyn had given the funeral director.

So they went to the condo complex to see if they could find Selvyn. But when they knocked on the door, no one answered. Proctor huffed and kicked the railing. He wanted to finish this case and move on with his life. He was used to getting fast results. He made quick, impetuous decisions. Blair didn't seem distracted. He set his palm on the small of Proctor's back and led him downstairs to the back of the condo complex.

"Where are we doing now?" Proctor asked. "He's obviously not home, or he's moved out and he's gone for good." He knew these male stripper types: here today, gone tomorrow. Just like his shifty business manager.

"To the pool."

"Why on Earth would I want to go to the pool in a low rent condominium complex? I don't even use my own pool very often."

Blair laughed. He stopped walking in the middle of a landing on a flight of steps that led down to a concrete lined community swimming pool. There was no one there to use the stained white vinyl chairs, except for a young man in a tight, sheer bathing suit. Blair gestured to the young man and said, "On a bright, sunny day like this, where else would I go to find a good looking young gay guy who lives in a low rent condo complex and works as a male stripper?"

77

Proctor glanced down at the young man. He was stretched out on a lounge chair, covered in grease, baking in the sun. "This is ridiculous. You don't know that's Selvyn Markowitz. Furthermore, it's awfully presumptuous, if not insulting, to all young gay men and male strippers to think that just because someone is young and gay, he's sitting by the pool working on his tan."

"Ha," Blair said, as he gently shoved Proctor down the steps. "You show me a pool in a low rent condo complex on a bright sunny day anywhere in Hollywood, and I'll find you a young queen with delusions of grandeur working on his beloved tan."

Proctor rolled his eyes. "That's so politically incorrect I'm not even going to dignify it with a reply. You are the crudest man I've ever met."

But when they approached the young man on the lounge chair and Blair said, "I'm looking for someone named Selvyn Markowitz," and the young man replied, "I'm Selvyn Markowitz," Proctor gulped and looked in the other direction to avoid eye contact with Blair. He hated it when Blair was always so right about everything.

Blair extended his hand and said, "I'm Blair Huntingdon, and this is my associate, Proctor Gamble. The funeral director who handled your late partner's service told us we could find you here."

Proctor remained silent. He could see Blair wanted to take control. But when Blair opened his mouth to speak again, Selvyn Markowitz pointed at Proctor and spoke over Blair. "I know *you*," he said. He sat up and gaped at Proctor. "You've been on TV, and magazine ads. I've seen your wet swimsuit poster everywhere. You're the famous model. I'm trying to be a famous model myself."

Proctor smiled, and sent Blair a glance. Blair been right on both counts: the model's delusions of grandeur *and* the sun worshiping. It was a painful cliché Proctor didn't like to face about other gay men. He pulled out a chair that was beneath a small garden table next to Selvyn's lounge chair, and said, "Yes, that's me. I guess I'll never live that wet underwear poster down. It's nice to meet you, Mr. Markowitz." He shook Selvyn's hand and sat down. "And this is my assistant, Blair Huntingdon. I'm sorry to hear about your loss. I know this is a terrible time to ask you questions, but it's really very important. Any information you could provide would be a huge help."

While Proctor took control, letting Blair know that he was just as capable of asking smart questions, Blair took a seat beside him and watched quietly.

Selvyn glanced at them both and stood up from the lounge chair. When he stood, he stretched his arms up as far as he could and grunted. The skimpy bathing suit he wore was so sheer it was impossible not to notice the bulging outline of his huge, thick penis. He was taller than Proctor would have guessed from seeing him on his back. He had dark hairy legs and a tight athletic build that suggested he worked out with weights quite often. Though he was nice looking in a rough trade sexy way, he wasn't model material. He seemed more than eager to show off his body—and his penis. When he finished stretching, he actually spread his legs right in front of them, reached into this bathing suit, and adjusted his balls without a hint of chagrin. Then he smiled at Proctor and said, "I'm sorry, but I hate being confined. If it weren't for the rules at this fucking condo association, I wouldn't be wearing anything. I like to sunbathe in the nude."

Blair crossed his legs and glanced down at his shoes.

Proctor said, "I know how tedious those things can be." He wasn't sure what else to say. The guy was standing there with his dick practically hanging out of his bathing suit, begging for attention. This was one of those times when Proctor wished some young gay men would work more on their self-esteem and less on their bodies and tans.

Selvyn pulled out a chair and sat beside Proctor. Before he sat, he made sure his dick brushed up against Proctor's shoulder.

Proctor glanced at Blair and rolled his eyes. Then he turned to Selvyn and said, "We're very sorry to bother you this way, especially while you're still grieving, but we'd like to ask you a few questions about a ring that belonged to your deceased partner, Dwayne Calvin."

Selvyn's arm went up and his wrist went limp. "Oh, that thing. Girl, I know exactly what you're talking about." His lisp became more pronounced as he started using campy feminine pronouns.

Though Proctor hated to be addressed with feminine pronouns, he smiled and said, "We'd like to ask you a few questions about the ring."

"We collect old jewelry," Blair said, then jabbed Proctor's ribs with his elbow.

Selvyn laughed and glanced down at Proctor's crotch. He moved his chair closer to Proctor's and set his hairy naked leg against Proctor's knee. He reached down again to adjust his dick and said, "I'm sorry, girl. That was supposed to be our ticket to freedom and wealth, ha-ha. But it's worthless and I don't know what happened to it."

From what Proctor could see without actually looking down between Selvyn's legs, he was almost fully erect and the head of his dick was sticking out of his bathing suit. "I see," he said, trying to focus on Selvyn's face instead of his crotch.

"Dwayne was wearing the ring while he was jogging that morning," Selvyn said. He reached into his bathing suit and pulled his dick all the way out. He smiled and said, "I hope you don't mind. For some reason I can't seem to control myself today. Sometimes my penis has a mind of its own. I'm ready to burst out of this bathing suit. And when you have a flagpole like this, it's hard to keep it down sometimes." Then he laughed and rubbed his leg against Proctor's.

Proctor pressed his palm to his throat and took a quick breath. Though he'd been with more men than he could count, he'd never been into men who made bold gestures like this in public. He didn't care how good looking they were or how well endowed. There was nothing in the definition of the word vulgar that piqued Proctor's interest.

"I know he was wearing the ring the morning he died," Selvyn said. "He always wore that ugly ring. It makes no sense. He never left the house without that worthless piece of shit on his finger."

Blair smiled at the way Selvyn's long penis rested on its side. He said, "He always wore the ring? Did you ask the police about it?"

Selvyn shrugged. His penis jumped and rested on his leg. "I didn't want to get involved with the police. I'd rather stay as far away from them as I can. It was his father's ring. The old man didn't have much else in life to leave Dwayne, which is why Dwayne wore it all the time. The father was a quirky old dude. He knew more about art and paintings than anyone I know. He passed away about a month before Dwayne got run over by the car."

"Isn't it unusual that Dwayne's father would leave him a worthless ring, especially if he knew so much about great art? It doesn't make sense." Proctor asked.

Selvyn smiled. A door slammed and two young women walked into the pool area. He quickly grabbed his erection and shoved it back into his bathing suit so he wouldn't get into trouble. He had trouble covering it; the head didn't fit and he had to rest his palm over the head to keep it concealed. "Nothing about that old man-made sense. If you knew Dwayne's father you wouldn't think it was unusual for him to have a worthless ring like that. Dwayne's grandfather was a fighter pilot during

World War II. Supposedly he was shot down over France by the Germans and he was held in a prison camp. While he was there, some old Nazi told him about a rare collection of paintings that had been hidden somewhere that were worth $5,000,000 back then. I think the artist's name was Pierre Bouvier."

Proctor's head went up. "I've heard about those lost paintings. Some think they don't exist. Pierre Bouvier was taken prisoner by the Nazis during World War II, put in a concentration camp, and killed because he was openly homosexual. To this day, his paintings have never been recovered."

Blair sent him a look. "How on Earth would you know something like that?"

Proctor rolled his eyes. "I read. I go to galleries. I have friends, both in New York and Los Angeles, in the art world."

Blair smiled. "Excuse me, Your Royal Highness."

Selvyn didn't seem interested in their banter. When the two young women crossed through the pool area and exited, he pulled his dick back out of his bathing suit and brushed a piece of lint off the smooth, thick shaft.

The lint landed on Proctor's thigh. He blinked and pretended he didn't see it.

"I'm sorry," Selvyn said, as he reached for the lint. He flicked it off Proctor's leg and said, "I must have washed this bathing suit with my socks. I've got these fuzzy things all over my cock today." He bucked his hips forward and smiled. "See what I mean?"

The best way to deal with someone like this was to ignore the overtures. So Proctor smiled and said, "About the ring?"

"From what I know, the Nazi soldier told Dwayne's grandfather where the paintings were hidden. The Nazi soldier told him to get them, bring them to America, and that he would contact him after the war. But when the war was over, Dwayne's grandfather screwed the old Nazi over. He fucked him royally." Selvyn laughed while he told this story, as if he didn't believe a word of it. "Dwayne's grandfather hid the collection in some secret place. He was waiting until it was safe, supposedly because the Nazi was always looking for it." Selvyn pronounced the word supposedly as "supposably."

Blair leaned forward. He ignored the way Selvyn started to slowly stroke his dick. "And you don't think the story is true, *supposably*?"

Proctor looked down and smiled. Blair could be vicious at times.

Selvyn sent Blair a sharp look, as if Blair were an idiot. "I'll bet no one has to tell you when it's time to come in out of cold." Then he sent Blair a frown and double snapped him.

Blair glanced between Selvyn's legs and stared at his exposed erection. "At least I know when to put my dick back into my pants, *girl*."

Proctor kicked Blair. He wanted him to shut up so Selvyn would keep talking. He knew he could get anything out of Selvyn. He wasn't very bright. He could also tell that Selvyn wasn't too fond of Blair.

Selvyn moved closer to Proctor and rested his hand on Proctor's upper thigh. He gazed into Proctor's eyes and said, "Of course that story isn't true. It's a goddamn fairy tale that's been handed down from one nutty father to two nutty sons. The grandfather lived in a dumpy little apartment and worked in the maintenance department of a large building in Los Angeles all his life. Dwayne's father lived in a trailer and worked in the same building, in the same maintenance department all his life. He studied fine art for pleasure at the public library and he never graduated from high school. If there had been millions of dollars in hidden paintings by Pierre Bouvier, I doubt they would have lived that way, working as maintenance men in a Los Angeles high rise. Dwayne was just as bad. He always said they were too scared to reveal where the paintings were hidden. Dwayne said he wouldn't reveal where they were hidden either, at least not until after his father was gone and he could figure out how to do it safely. That's why Dwayne never really amounted to much in life. He was always dreaming about this fortune. He worked a few part time jobs, including maintenance a few days a week in the high rise building downtown where his father worked. For some reason, working in maintenance in that building was a family tradition with all of them. He jogged every morning.

"And, like his father and grandfather, Dwayne was a professional pilot who never did anything to make money at it. I honestly don't even think he liked flying much and I was never sure why he bothered. He used to get paid to go to these parties as a guest in Beverly Hills. Sometimes he stripped in clubs for extra cash. But he spent most of the time fucking, jogging, and sleeping, waiting for his father to drop dead so he could get his hands on the paintings and figure out how to make millions with them."

"And the father died a month before Dwayne," Proctor said.

"Almost to the day," Selvyn said. He pressed his palm to his throat and laughed. "And get this, a few days after the father dropped dead, some guy knocks on the door and offers Dwayne 20 grand for that goddamn piece-of-shit ring. It was the only thing the old fool left Dwayne. He didn't even leave him money for a burial. I paid for both funerals myself. But Dwayne wouldn't sell the ring. He said it meant too much to him and that it was all he had left of his father. I wanted to kick him in the ass. We could have used that in a big way to start our lives. I want to get new pec implants to make my chest bigger." He sat up and squared his back. He flexed his chest muscles and made them jiggle up and down. "I guess I can live with these, but I'd like bigger ones someday. I strip part time in a club in Hollywood. Guys like big pecs and big dicks on strippers. I'd make more money in tips."

Proctor immediately thought of the Prince. "Was the guy who offered you the $20,000 about 45, tall, dark hair? And did he have a tall blond assistant with him? A big guy with a crooked face and huge, bulging muscles?"

"No, the guy who came here asking about the ring was short and bald. She was old, girl. She had that old skin, girl. She wore a tweed sport jacket and reminded me of someone's grandfather. And believe me, I'd remember if two tall guys came here and offered me $20,000, especially if one was a blond with huge muscles. If they came here now, I'd bend over and do anything they wanted me to do, you can bet on that. You don't find that kind of money in the street every day."

"I'll bet you would do anything to please a man," Blair said with a snide grin.

Selvyn stood up and stretched, with his exposed erection sticking out in plain sight for everyone to see. He ignored Blair and moved closer to Proctor. When his erection was only about an inch from Proctor's lips, he looked down and asked, "Why don't you take off your clothes and we'll go for a swim?" He turned his back completely on Blair. "I'd love to see what you look like in person with wet underwear. We can make out in the pool." His voice went soft with a more effeminate tone.

Before Proctor had a chance to reply, Blair stood up and reached for Selvyn's arm. He gently moved him away from Proctor and said, "Sorry, buddy, he doesn't have time for a swim. We have a boat to catch at the airport. Besides, he doesn't wear underwear." Then he reached down, took Proctor's hand and yanked him up out of the chair.

Though Proctor didn't like being pulled around by anyone, he couldn't complain this time. He had no interest in swimming or making out with Selvyn Markowitz.

It was lucky someone else entered the pool area at the exact moment Blair yanked Proctor out of the chair, because it forced Selvyn to put his dick back into his bathing suit fast, and allowed Blair and Proctor to make a quick exit. They shook Selvyn's hand, thanked him for his help, and wished him luck. Then they turned and headed back to the steps that would lead them to the street before Selvyn had a chance to expose himself again.

When they were out on the street, Blair opened the passenger door for Proctor and held it for him. Proctor hadn't expected him to do this, but he didn't say anything. He never expected guys to do this for other guys. He certainly wouldn't have held the door open for Blair or for any other man, for that matter. But Blair seemed to do these little things in such an unplanned, natural way it didn't seem to matter much.

As Proctor climbed into the car, he said, "This is all about millions of dollars' worth of lost art, by a famous French artist who was killed by Nazis for being homosexual." He didn't expect a reply; he was talking out loud to himself. He'd read about the gay French artist, Pierre Bouvier, and he'd absorbed the legend of his lost paintings without forming a final opinion. Some seemed to think it was all legend, while others seemed to agree it was fact.

Blair replied anyway. "If Dwayne's father and grandfather were telling the truth, we now have a better plan." Then he shut the door and crossed to the other side of the car.

When he sat down, he said, "Now all we have to do is find the lost paintings before anyone else and hand them over to the French government." He adjusted his seat, then turned and leaned over. He grabbed Proctor's neck and pulled Proctor's face toward his. He started to kiss Proctor for no apparent reason.

Proctor hadn't expected the kiss. He had a feeling Blair was jealous of the way Selvyn had behaved and he wanted to reclaim his territory. Though Proctor was not used to kissing men on a public street, surrounded by people and cars, he didn't pull back. There was something soft and comforting about kissing Blair and made his knees go weak. It was more than sexual, and it filled him with so much emotion he had trouble containing himself.

Then Blair stopped kissing him and jerked back fast. He became stiff and stared through the windshield without speaking.

Proctor was hard by then and he wanted more. He reached between Blair's legs, grabbed his balls, and said, "Why did you stop? I was ready to hop into the back seat and take off my pants." He knew this was wrong, especially because he had no intention of getting seriously involved with Blair. But one more time certainly couldn't hurt either of them.

Blair continued to stare straight ahead. "While it sounds very tempting, I don't think you want to get into the backseat and take off your pants, or anything else, for that matter."

"Why are you staring that way? What's wrong? You're freaking me out."

"I'm going to tell you something, but you have to promise to remain calm," Blair said. He thought for a moment, then opened the car door. "On second thought, we're getting out of here." He climbed out of the car and jogged to the passenger side.

When he opened the door, he grabbed Proctor's wrist and said, "Let's go."

"Where?"

"I can't tell you. We just have to leave…right now. We'll rent a car and come back for this one later."

"I'm not leaving the car here," Proctor said. "I'm not going anywhere until you tell me what's wrong."

"Why do you always have to be so damn difficult?"

"I'm not moving a muscle." He set his jaw and laced his fingers together on his lap.

Blair bit his bottom lip. "Okay, but you have to promise me you won't get excited."

"Okay, I won't get excited." This was getting tired. For such a butch guy, he certainly could be high strung at times.

Blair took a deep breath. "Remember the Prince?"

"Yes. How could I forget the way he burned my salami?"

"He's in the backseat and he's dead. Don't look." He grabbed Proctor's head so he couldn't turn it sideways.

Proctor gulped. "He's dead?"

"His mouth is hanging open, his eyes are glaring, his lips are blue, and he doesn't seem to be breathing. I'm no expert, but I think that means he's dead."

Proctor took a quick look. The second he turned, the Prince's body moved sideways and fell across the back seat. He was dead all right. His face was blue and his eyes were wide open. Proctor pressed his palm to his chest and gasped. This was the second dead person he'd seen up close, and this time it was worse. He reached for Blair's hand, screamed, and jumped out of the car with such force he landed on Blair, with his arms around Blair's shoulders and his legs wrapped about Blair's waist.

"Get down," Blair said in a low voice, trying not to attract attention. "We have to get out of here and not attract attention." He pushed Proctor off his body and they started walking away from the car.

"We can't just leave."

"Oh, yes, we can. Someone is giving us a sign. They are letting us know we're being watched."

"*Who?*"

"How the hell should I know?"

"That's it. I've had it. I'm not playing games anymore, Blair. I'm taking the ring to the police, I'm giving it to them, and I'm closing down this agency like I should have done."

He walked so fast Blair seemed to have trouble keeping up with him. Blair reached for his arm and said, "Please don't. This is a huge case. It will put us on the map. I'll take care of you and everything will be okay. I promise I will. Just don't do anything without thinking just when we're starting to get somewhere with this case."

Proctor didn't slow down. He turned a corner, refusing to listen to another word Blair said. Two dead guys in one week were enough for him. Two dead guys in one lifetime would have been enough for him a month earlier. How could he have let his charmed life come down to this? When he thought about all he'd lost and how hard he would have to work to get it back, he wanted to kick something until it was broken. At least there was time to get out of this mess with Blair and this idiotic detective agency, before it went any further. What kind of idiot would name a detective agency Exotique, anyway? It sounded more like a brothel. There was nothing Blair could say or do this time that would change his mind.

Chapter Nine

Procter tried to call a taxi on his cell phone but couldn't get a decent signal on the street. Blair was still following him, shouting for him to stop. He had never been to this part of town before on foot and wasn't sure where to go, so he saw a sign above a door that read *Athletic Club*, and pushed the doors open. He walked into a small, quiet lobby with gray walls and a darker gray carpet and glanced around. He wondered what kind of athletic club this was because there didn't seem to be any people walking around in workout clothing. The soft music in the background wasn't the high energy type of drum pounding he was used to hearing at the gym where he went on occasion in Beverly Hills. This music was soft and slow, almost like the music he listened to in his dentist's office. The only human there was an old man sitting behind a tall counter that was stacked with white towels.

When Blair came rushing through the door, Proctor tried to use his phone again. But now he saw the phone needed to be charged, which was why he couldn't call on the street. He turned right and saw a pay phone next to a tall plastic potted palm tree. He hadn't used a pay phone in years; he was surprised to see pay phones were actually still around in some places. This one looked old, too, like a nostalgic remnant from the 1980s. When he turned his back on Blair and started fishing through his pockets for change, all he came up with was cash and a handful of nickels.

Blair rested his palm on Proctor's shoulder and asked, "What are you doing now?"

"My phone needs a charge and I'm trying to call the police," Proctor said. "I want this to stop right now. I can't take any more. I'm afraid I'll be the next one to wind up dead in the backseat of a car. I'm not cut out for this line of work, Blair. I can't take it anymore."

Blair pulled his own phone out of his pocket and handed it to Proctor. He remained expressionless, and spoke in a low voice. "If you feel this way, use my phone. I don't think that pay phone is real. I think it's just a decoration. I'm not going to stop you. I don't want to see you unhappy. You're too pretty to frown. I just wanted to take advantage of what could be a great thing for my career as a detective and for Exotique. I wasn't doing this just for me. I was doing it for US. We're both kind of lost right now."

Proctor removed his hands from his pockets and took Blair's phone. Before he dialed, he said, "That's another thing I've been meaning to mention. Who on Earth would take the name Exotique Private Detective Agency seriously? It sounds like a whorehouse. I know I wouldn't take it seriously if I were looking for a private detective."

Blair seemed slightly offended, but tried hard not to show it. "I thought it was kind of catchy, myself. I wanted something that would stand out and be tasteful at the same time. But if you'd rather change the name, I'm fine with that. I'd like to see if *you* can come up with anything better."

Proctor rolled his eyes. "A five year old could come up with a better name than that, idiot." He thought for a moment. "I'm not interested in changing the name. All I want to do is close it all down and get out before I lose any more money…or get my throat slit. But if I were going to rename the agency, I'd choose something like The Rainbow Detective Agency, to show that it's proudly owned by respectable, politically correct, LGBT people, not a freaking pimp."

Blair rubbed his jaw and considered this for a moment. "I kind of like that…The Rainbow Detective Agency. I'll have the sign on the door changed immediately."

He never gave up. Proctor dialed 911 and said, "Forget it, Blair. It's too late. I'm calling the police and I'm giving them the ring. They can deal with this now."

"Please think about this," Blair said. "It's the most important case I've ever had. And it's great experience for you to learn the business. Please don't do this to *us*. You're making a huge mistake."

Though Proctor hated to see Blair beg, he couldn't take another minute of all this insanity. When the 911 dispatcher answered, Proctor told her it was very important and he had to speak to the police. But the dispatcher put him on hold and started playing annoying music.

Blair took advantage of the pause and said, "If you just give me a chance I know I can figure all this out. I think the engraving on the bottom of the ring has something to do with where the lost paintings were hidden. It's some kind of code. I just have to break it."

"No," Proctor said, while the annoying Muzak version *Puff The Magic Dragon* started to play in his ear. "You're not going to talk me out of it this time. I've been a fool to have gone this far."

"Just listen to reason for a minute, that's all I ask."

"No," said Proctor. Then the phone clicked and he lost the call. "I can't believe I can't even get the police. This is a fucking nightmare."

"Look, I'll take you back to the office and you can think about it tonight. You'll be able to make a more rational decision tomorrow after you've slept on it."

"Oh no," Proctor said. "I'm handing that ring over to the police, and then I'm taking a taxi to the Beverly Hills hotel. I'm getting a bungalow and I'm sleeping in a nice warm bed tonight, not in an office on a hard leather sofa." He lifted the phone higher and started dialing again.

"Are you calling the police again?" Blair asked.

"No, I'm calling a taxi. I'll go the police station in person, and then I'm going to Beverly Hills."

Blair lowered his eyes and reached for the phone. He took it out of Proctor's hand, turned it off, and stared at him for a long time.

Though Proctor could see how serious Blair was about saving the agency, he had to be strong. So Proctor looked into his eyes without blinking and said, "Give me the ring so I can take it to the police, Blair. It's over."

This time Blair seemed to understand Proctor wasn't joking anymore. He hesitated for a moment, then pulled the ring out of his pants pocket and set it in Proctor's palm. Blair glanced at the old man behind the counter and said, "Would you call a taxi for the gentleman?"

The old man nodded and made the phone call.

When Proctor saw the pained expression on Blair's face, he lowered his voice and said, "Thank you." He put the ring into his back pocket where it would be safe.

Blair shrugged. "No problem."

The old man at the counter put down the phone and said, "It's going to be about 25 minutes, they said."

Proctor clenched his fists and looked up at the ceiling. "Twenty-five minutes?"

The old man shrugged without offering a reason why it would be so long, and went back to something he was reading. He didn't seem to care one way or the other.

Blair smiled and said, "We'll make it go by fast. I'll rent a room."

"A room?" Proctor glanced around. It didn't look like a hotel.

Blair smiled. "We're in a bathhouse."

"The sign said athletic club."

Blair sighed and exhaled. "I thought you knew."

"How the hell would I know something like that?" Proctor said. "I don't hang out in *this* part of town." Though Proctor had always been curious about bathhouses, he'd never actually been to one.

"We have 25 minutes, give or take," Blair said. "We may as well get a room and have a little fun, for old time's sake." He reached around and grabbed Proctor's ass hard. "You know you want it."

Proctor smiled. "You're a sick man with one thing on your dirty mind."

"Sue me."

Proctor couldn't stand out on the street waiting for the next 25 minutes, or longer. He couldn't stand there in the lobby of a bathhouse either. There was no telling who might walk in and come after him. So he told the man at the desk to make the taxi wait, he let Blair get a "standard" room for a half hour, and then he followed Blair into long dimly lit hallway off the reception area. On the way to the room, they passed a portly middle-aged man wearing nothing but a towel and a great big silly grin. He was scratching his nuts and licking his thin lips. Proctor looked down at his shoes. When the man reached out to touch Proctor, Blair grabbed his wrist and said, "Off limits, buddy. He's all mine."

At that time of day, the place wasn't very crowded. The handful of men who were there all looked the same: graying hair, bushy eyebrows, slight paunches, and leering eyes. It was as if they were waiting for Proctor to make eye contact so they could swoop in for the kill. Though Blair was attractive, they didn't do this to him. They seemed to sense Proctor was more submissive at a glance. With Blair, they sensed he was more dominant and left him alone. For this reason, it wasn't the kind of place Proctor would ever visit alone. But he had to admit being there with Blair made him feel safer. He could absorb things that normally would have made him panic and run.

When they found their room at the end of the dark hallway, Blair walked over to a twin bed and started removing his tie. "Take it all off and we'll go into the sauna for a few minutes. Doesn't look crowded here today."

"I thought we were going to just stay here, in the room," Proctor said.

"Nonsense," Blair said. "Half the fun is getting naked and walking around in front of the other guys, especially if you have someone to do it with. Now, shut up and take it all off."

Proctor kicked off his shoes. "You seem awfully familiar with places like this."

Blair pulled down his zipper and smiled. "I've been a few times. I'm no saint."

When they were both naked, Blair walked up to Proctor and kissed him on the cheek. He ran his hand down the side of his face and said, "You're gorgeous even in this bad lighting." Then he reached for Proctor's hand and two white towels he'd just rolled up on the bed. They exited the room naked, with the rolled towels under Blair's arm, and headed down the dark hall to a small sauna room with wooden benches.

There were two other guys in the sauna. They were younger than the other men Proctor had seen so far. They appeared to be in their mid-20s. Both had dark hair and slim bodies, and both had hairy legs and heavy five o-clock shadow. Even though it was darker in the sauna than it had been in the hall, it would have been impossible to miss them making out and stroking their dicks at the same time. Proctor gaped at their huge erections and their lack of concern. Both were so into what they were doing they didn't even turn to see who had entered.

For a moment, Proctor felt awkward and he reached for Blair's arm. "I'm not sure about this. Those guys are having sex over there right in front of us, or anyone else that wants to watch. I've never done anything like this before." Proctor had done three-ways with other guys in the privacy of his own home or someone else's. He'd once taken on three guys in a hotel room in Amsterdam. But he'd never seen or done anything in such a public place before. He wasn't worried about being recognized by anyone. The world knew him as openly gay; they wouldn't be shocked. Besides, most of the people who went to places like this shunned publicity and craved discretion themselves.

Blair grabbed his ass and said, "You'll love it, trust me. This is what's supposed to happen in places like this. It's like the last place left on Earth where guys like us can be ourselves. No one can judge us, point fingers at us, tell us what is right and wrong, and offer unsolicited opinions about what gay men are supposed to do or how they are supposed to behave. It's priceless and it's disappearing, so you'd better enjoy what little there is left of it right now while you still have a chance. Unless you'd rather go home and bake YUMMY cookies and post cute pictures of kitty cats and puppy dogs and on Facebook." Then he tossed the towels on a bench near the door and guided Proctor to another bench not far from where the two young guys were making out.

When they were seated, it didn't take long for Blair to lean over and wrap his arms around Proctor. He kissed him hard and Proctor's body went back against the wooden bench so far his head landed only inches away from the young guys who were making out. The two young strangers kissing and tugging at their dicks didn't seem to mind. When Blair climbed on top of Proctor and pinned him to the bench, one of the guys leaned over and started to suck the other guy's dick. The guy who was getting sucked off spread his legs wider, leaned back, and rested his thigh against the top of Proctor's head. They were so close Proctor could smell the deodorant they'd used that morning. When he took a deeper breath, he could smell the damp aroma between their legs.

For a while, the only sounds in the sauna room came from Proctor and Blair kissing and the wet slurps from the young guy sucking the other one's dick. Proctor was hard by then and he felt a surge of excitement pass through his body. He wasn't going to have sex with the other guys; he only wanted Blair, no one else. But being in the same room while the other guys were having sex caused Proctor's heart to pound so fast he had to concentrate on his breathing so he wouldn't hyperventilate. When he thought about the way he was making out with Blair in front of the other guys, he lifted his legs and wrapped them around Blair's waist.

At one point, while Blair was still kissing Proctor and Proctor was playing with Blair's dick, one young guy said to the other, "Get up and sit on my cock, man. I wanna fuck you." He spoke in a low voice, but loud enough for Proctor and Blair to hear.

When the young guy said this, Blair climbed off Proctor's body and said, "Get up, I want you to sit on my lap, too." He glanced at the young guy on the bench and said, "We'll fuck them both at the same time, man." Then he crossed to where he'd left the towels and pulled out a condom. He must have rolled the condom up in the towel before they'd left the room and Proctor hadn't noticed.

By the time Blair returned, he had a condom on his cock and he was holding his balls. The one young guy was already on the other guy's lap and he was guiding a large dick into his hole. Proctor stood still, watching the two young guys, noticing they used condoms, too, waiting for Blair's next move. Blair set his hand on Proctor's ass and guided him to the bench. Blair sat down first, only inches away from where the young guys were. Then he stretched out his legs and leaned back exactly like the young guy who was sitting on the bench next to him. Blair tapped his leg and smiled. He grabbed his dick and said, "Climb aboard, baby."

Proctor smiled at Blair's cheesy sarcasm. He stepped forward, faced Blair, and climbed up on his lap. He straddled Blair's dick just like the other guy had straddled his partner's dick. He spread his legs, his knees resting on the wooden bench. He reached around and guided the head into his opening. He slowly sat down on it, holding Blair's shoulders like the other guy was holding his partner's shoulders. By the time Blair was deep inside, Proctor glanced to the right and made eye contact with the guy who was sitting on his partner's dick. This was the first time he'd actually made eye contact with either of them. The guy was better looking up close, in that skater boy, unshaven, messy way that seemed so popular lately. He was rocking his hips slowly, with his back arched, while the other guy's dick was deep inside him. He sent Proctor a deep stare with dark brown eyes and said, "You guys are hot, man." Then he leaned over and kissed Proctor on the mouth.

Proctor's hips moved forward. He clamped down on Blair's shaft and said, "So are you guys."

The guy smiled again. He squeezed Proctor's left chest muscle. "Let's give these boys a ride they'll never forget."

Blair grabbed Proctor's waist and said, "Ride that dick, baby. Show these guys who knows how to fuck better." He slapped Proctor's ass. It made a loud crack.

The guy next to Blair slapped his partner's ass and laughed. "You should see this one ride dick. He's a fucking pro, man."

Proctor glanced at the other guy and smiled. No one knew how to ride a cock better than Proctor, at least in his opinion. The other guy returned the smile and they both started moving their hips faster, as if they were in a grinding competition. The door cracked and two more guys entered the sauna to see what was going on. Proctor saw them sit down on the opposite side, about two feet apart. They removed their towels and spread their legs, preparing for a double feature. Proctor forgot about them and continued to ride as fast as the younger guy. He bounced up and down on Blair's lap, and the bottom of his ass slapped against Blair's legs. Blair's erection slid in and out of his body, going deeper and harder each time he went down. Proctor only glanced back over his shoulder once again to see what the guys on the other side of the sauna were doing. They were both in their late thirties, and both had nice bodies with hairy chests. They gaped at the two couples having sex in public, with their eyes glazed and their lips parted, slowly stroking, never once making any contact with each other.

It didn't take long for Blair and the other guy sitting on the bench to moan they were close to climax. Blair and the other guy leaned into each other, shoulders touching, and extended their legs. The one guy told his partner, "Fuck, man, I'm coming." When he said this, Blair squeezed Proctor's waist and whispered, "I'm gonna blast, too, baby. Don't stop." He started to slam into Proctor's ass from below.

Blair and the guy next to him rode faster. They held their own dicks and jacked. A minute or two later, Blair's body tightened and he blasted the condom. A second after that, the guy leaning against Blair's shoulder started to repeat the word fuck in a deep whisper and he came next. Then the guy riding the other guy's dick reached for Proctor's arm. He held Proctor for support with one hand and jacked off his own load with the other. Proctor came an instant later, shooting come all over Blair's chest.

When Proctor heard the two guys on the other side of the sauna get up and leave, he didn't look back this time. He was too engrossed in what he was doing to care. He figured they got off and decided to exit now that the show was over. Proctor didn't care about them; he only cared about what was still deep inside his body and he wanted to enjoy every last inch of it. He leaned forward and kissed Blair on the lips a second before the other guy did the same thing to his partner. Both couples made out a minute or two longer, with each other and themselves, leaning into each other, rubbing shoulders, legs, and arms. It was exciting for Proctor to make out with these hot young guys while Blair was still inside him. But he didn't get the same jolt of energy from them that he received when he kissed Blair.

When they all stopped kissing, the younger guy climbed off his partner's lap first. He kissed Proctor on the cheek and said, "You guys are hot. Do you come here often?"

Proctor smiled and said, "No, we've never been here before together. This was our first time."

The guy who had been sitting on the bench the entire time next to Blair grabbed his dick and said, "We should all take a shower together now." He smiled at Proctor, leaned forward, and patted his ass. He was the aggressive top guy. "Maybe after that we can take turns and you can sit on my lap for a while. Or me and your buddy here can bend you guys over and take turns tagging each of you over a bench." He rubbed Proctor's ass and bit his lip. "I'd like to get in *there*."

Though Proctor was always flattered when a younger guy made an advance, he wasn't interested in taking turns. Twenty-five minutes had to have gone by, and the taxi was probably out front waiting for him. So he climbed off Blair's dick and said, "I wish we could. But we have to leave now. See you guys later." Then he turned, reached for a towel, and left Blair sitting on the bench.

By the time Blair caught up with him, he already had his pants on and he was about to put on his shirt. Blair walked up to him, put his arms around him, and kissed him so hard he almost fell back onto the twin bed. Blair's hands went up and down his body. He squeezed his ass and crotch and legs.

When Blair finally stopped kissing, Proctor had to concentrate to keep his balance. He'd never been kissed in a way that made his jaw hurt before, and he'd never felt such a shock of energy pass through his entire body. But he knew what Blair was doing. Blair wanted him to keep working on this case. Blair was smooth but transparent. Only Proctor just wasn't cut out to live a life like this.

While Blair put on his pants without saying a word, Proctor buttoned his shirt and put on his socks and shoes. He walked over to Blair and reached for his hand. "I'm leaving now. Are you going to be okay?" Now that he knew he'd probably never see him again, he wanted to part on good terms. He'd always insisted on remaining friendly with all of his ex-lovers.

Blair smiled. "I'll be fine. I promise. You be safe now."

This was harder than Proctor thought it would be. He knew he had to turn and leave, but his legs didn't want to move. "Are you sure?"

Blair kissed him gently on the lips and said, "I'm sure. You go on, I'll be fine. I'm a big boy and I know how to take care of myself."

Proctor turned and slowly walked to the door. He opened it, took a step into the hall, and stopped. He turned back and smiled at Blair. "Thank you for giving me the ring so I can take it to the police. I know how important this case was to you. But someday you'll see this was the right thing to do. You'll thank me."

Blair returned the smile. He didn't seem as upset as Proctor would have guessed a half hour earlier. "Stop worrying about me. I'm a survivor, baby. I know how to take care of myself."

Proctor nodded. "I want you to know that even though I've complained, I actually did have a lot of fun with you. I think this has been the most exciting couple of days of my entire life. I just wanted you to know that before I go."

"Me, too, baby," Blair said. "I'll never forget you." He buckled his belt and adjusted his tie. Evidently, he wasn't going to turn this goodbye into warm tender moment. Some men just didn't have that kind of emotion no matter how hard they tried.

"I guess I'll be going then," Proctor said. He couldn't understand what was wrong with him. He'd never been one of those people who didn't know when to leave. He could see now that Blair understood. It was time to go back to his real life. Yet, for some reason, he couldn't seem to make his legs move.

"Take care," Blair said. "I'll be seeing you."

On his way out, the man at the desk told Proctor the taxi had been waiting outside for almost 20 minutes with the meter running. Proctor thanked him and said it was fine. As he left the building, a wave of disappointment came over him and he wasn't sure why. Though he should have been thrilled he was finally going to see all this detective business end, he felt nothing but emptiness right down to the bottom of his stomach.

Chapter Ten

The next morning Procter kicked a chair in the hotel room so hard he thought he broke his toe. He dressed so fast he forgot about the pain and didn't even bother to check the back of his head to be sure his hair was in place. It had been years since Proctor had driven so fast and parked with such alacrity, especially since it was an unfamiliar rental car. On the way over from the Beverly Hills Hotel, he bit the inside of his mouth and gripped the steering wheel until his knuckles turned white. He skidded into the first open parking space and left the car on a slant in perfect alignment with those surrounding his. Then he jumped out of the car, slammed the door so hard it echoed through the indoor parking garage, and stomped to the elevator. He pushed the button hard, two or three times. When the elevator landed on the same floor as the detective agency, he heaved through a crowd of people and wended his way to Blair Huntingdon's office.

At the entrance of the office, he gaped at the glass doors and lifted his fists. There was a man in a white work suit repainting the sign on the glass from The Exotique Private Detective Agency to The Rainbow Private Detective Agency. Proctor took one look at what the painter was doing and shook his fists in mid-air. Then he gently moved the man aside without being aggressive, grabbed a rag from a bucket on the floor, and wiped the newly painted letters into a huge blotchy smear. If Blair Huntingdon thought Proctor was playing games, Blair Huntingdon was sadly mistaken. No one made a fool out of Proctor this many times without paying for it.

By the time he stormed into the reception area, his face was red and he had to control his temper so he wouldn't scream at innocent people. That poor unfortunate young guy was sitting behind the reception desk out front: Alvin Schlock. Poor Alvin was on the phone again, speaking with that painful wrecked voice, flashing that goofy buck toothed smile.

He had the largest teeth Proctor had ever seen. It made Proctor wince to imagine Alvin eating a club sandwich. Alvin was wearing some kind of green plaid sweater vest that day, and a yellow bowtie against an electric blue dress shirt. It was such a bad color combination it caused a pull in Proctor's stomach. When Alvin spotted Proctor opening the glass door, he hung up the phone, turned, and started telling all the other employees that Proctor had arrived.

As Proctor entered, the other employees all stopped what they were doing and turned to face him. They smiled and applauded, and a few jumped up and down. Alvin Schlock said, "You have no idea how much it means to all of us here that you've decided to become part of the agency. And we love the new name, even the straight people who work here don't have a problem with the word *rainbow*. We think it's perfect."

Proctor held his tongue and glared at poor Alvin. How could he get mad at someone so pitiful and sweet? "I want to see Blair Huntingdon right now." Even though they were all applauding, the only thing Proctor could visualize was his right-hand squeezing Blair's nuts until he brought him to the floor writhing in pain. This time Blair had gone too far. This time Blair had done something to him he'd never forgive or forget.

Alvin Schlock seemed so excited he could barely contain his emotions. He continued to gush and thank Proctor, at one point wiping a tear of happiness from his left eye. So Proctor turned and headed back to Blair's office on his own. As he passed the cheering employees, he felt his chest cave in. Then all the blood in his body seemed to rush to his head. Blair had misled all these good, decent people into believing their jobs were safe, and nothing could have been farther from the truth. Now Proctor would have to be the bad guy and Blair would come off looking like a dejected hero.

When he reached Blair's office, he grabbed the handles and pulled hard to open the doors, only it was a push instead of pull entrance, and he wound up getting even more frustrated with Blair. So he kicked the door and pounded inside without warning. Blair was sitting behind his desk surrounded by stacks of papers, in front of his computer screen, sucking a pencil. Proctor crossed to the front of the desk and slammed both hands on it.

Blair didn't flit or flitter. He didn't jump or jerk. He looked up from a paper and smiled, with the same cool, casual, smug expression Proctor had grown to know. "Good morning, baby."

"Good morning? Is that all you have to say?"

"You're not smiling," Blair said. "And it's such a gorgeous day outside. You have to learn to stop and smell the roses. Life's short and all that sweet shit, you know."

"Don't you tell me what life is like?" Proctor said.

"I take it you're not in a good mood today. Why don't you just get down on your knees and suck my dick."

"You're lucky I didn't bring a fucking baseball bat with me," said Proctor. "Trust me, the last thing you want this morning are my teeth anywhere near to your dick."

Blair smiled. "That doesn't *parse*."

Proctor lifted his fists. "Don't fuck around with me, Blair. I'm in no mood for your shit."

They started speaking over each other and nothing made sense. Blair remained calm and continued to smile. He talked about how much everyone in the office loved Proctor and how Proctor had saved them all by deciding to keep the agency open. While Blair rambled on, making very little sense, Proctor ranted about how sneaky Blair was to have tricked him. Blair had led Proctor to believe he had the ring. Proctor wasn't certain exactly when it had happened, but at some point, while they were in the bathhouse the day before, Blair had taken the ring back.

The more Blair smiled, the louder Proctor shouted. "I want that ring back now, so I can take it to the police. Your tricked me, Blair."

Blair shrugged. "I can't give it to you. I'm only doing this for your own good. You'll ruin our business and everything we've planned so far. This is our future."

Proctor glanced down and reached for the first heavy object he saw. He lifted a large, ornamental black marble box with both hands and leaned back to get as much leverage as possible so that when he threw the box it would land on Blair's head. "We don't have a business," Proctor said. "And we don't have any plans for a future, you asshole. Where on Earth do you come up with these things?"

"Temper, temper," Blair said, still smiling. "If you throw that stone box, you could hurt someone—namely, *me*. I like my face. I think you like my face, too. At least that's the impression I get whenever you're sucking my face."

Proctor gritted his teeth. "*I want that ring.*" He hadn't been this angry since the time that younger male model stood in his light and tried to upstage him on a photo shoot and he wound up shoving the pushy, sneaky little fucker off the side of a boat in Newport.

Blair stood up and leaned forward, attempting to take the box from Proctor's hands. "Now be a good boy and give that to me. I don't want you to hurt yourself, and I don't want you to hurt me either. I'll make you a nice cup of herbal organic tea. You'll be a new man."

Without thinking, Proctor leaned back and hurled the stone box in Blair's direction. Blair turned sideways and threw up his arms. The box flew over his black leather office chair and crashed into the plate glass window behind him. Blair walked to the window, remaining calm and collected, and glanced down to see where the box had landed. "Good thing those hedgerows were planted in that spot to soften the fall. That could have been ugly."

Proctor lifted a tall, thin red glass vase next. "This time, stand still and I'll get *you* instead."

Blair crossed to the other side of the desk and yanked the red vase out of his hands. He set it down on the desk and said, "Okay, calm down. One broken window is enough for one day."

"I don't want to calm down," Proctor said. He punched a chair next to the desk. "I want that ring."

Blair put his arm around him and led him to the black leather sofa. He sat him down, and sat next to him, so close he was almost on Proctor's lap. Though Proctor was still angry about being deceived, his heart started to slow down and he began to breathe easier. Proctor wasn't an angry man by nature. He preferred to be calm and serene at all times, and he liked his life simple and quiet. When he was this close to Blair it was difficult to remain mad for long, especially with the way Blair had his arm around his shoulders.

"I've been working all night," Blair said. "Wait until you hear what I've come up with. You'll be glad I swiped that ring back yesterday when I was squeezing your ass."

"What are you talking about?" Proctor's voice went down and he took a quick breath. He was trying to relax. He didn't want to get angry again.

"I'm certain the engraving on the bottom of the ring is some kind of code," Blair said. He moved closer and pulled Proctor up against his chest. He kissed the top of Proctor's head and said, "I've been going over the engraved numbers all night. I've entered them into the computer, I've turned them around in every way I can, and I've come to one conclusion."

Proctor inhaled his tweedy scent and asked, "What conclusion?" He figured he might as well ask, and it wasn't just because he liked being held in Blair's arms this way. Although he didn't mention it to Blair, he'd been thinking about the engraving on the ring that night, too. For some reason, he couldn't get the damn ring and the lost Pierre Bouvier paintings out of his head. Everything had always come easily for Proctor. He'd become famous by accident, thanks to the wet underwear poster. Although he hadn't been born into privilege or money, he'd become wealthy without even knowing it was happening. He knew he'd never be a doctor, a lawyer, or anyone important who would make a huge difference in the world. Sometimes, late at night, this realization would bring him down to a point so low he wasn't sure he'd come back. And now, for the first time in his adult life, he finally felt challenged. But more than that, he felt as if he was doing something that might make a difference in the world—at least in the art world, and for all those people outside in the front office.

Blair's right hand went down and rested on the small of his back. "I remembered something Dwayne Calvin's creepy big dicked lover said yesterday next to the cheesy condo pool. He said that Dwayne, his father, and the grandfather were all pilots. I have a feeling the engraving is some kind of code or system that pilots would understand. I think the numbers in the engraving are longitude and latitude that point to where the lost paintings were hidden. The ring is worthless. It never meant anything to Dwayne, his father, or the grandfather...except for what's engraved beneath it. And that happens to be nothing other than a system, with respect to geographical locations as to how they relate to longitude and latitude."

Proctor frowned. "I'm lost. I have no idea what you're talking about." Anything that involved numbers had always passed him by, unless it pertained to money.

Blair's hand went lower. He slipped his palm into the back of Proctor's pants and said, "No underpants? Any location on Earth can be figured out by a set of numbers. I have a feeling the numbers on the engraving will lead us to the lost paintings." He started to squeeze Proctor's ass. Proctor's waistband popped and his zipper went down. Blair leaned forward and took a deep breath. "You smell good today, like you've been soaking in a tub all night."

There was no denying the energy between them. Proctor arched his back and his jeans slid down his thighs. Blair's fingers were now buried deep in his ass and Proctor was fully erect. He hadn't forgotten why he'd been angry; he just didn't want to think about it anymore. He shrugged and said, "When I checked into the Beverly Hills Hotel last night, I took a long, hot bubble bath, and another one this morning. It helps me relax. I've been so stressed out lately, I jump at the slightest sound."

Blair inserted his middle finger and kissed Proctor gently on the lips. While his finger moved, he bit Proctor's ear and said, "I'd like to take a long hot bath with you, baby. I know how to calm you down." He inserted another finger and began to probe very slowly.

By this time Proctor's legs were wide open and he was leaning all the way back on the sofa. "We have to stop this. Someone could walk in on us. There are people out there I've never met before cheering my name and clapping. What would they think?"

Blair shoved both fingers as deeply into Proctor's ass as he could get them. Then he leaned over and grabbed a phone on the coffee table with his other hand. He lifted the phone and said, "Hold all calls and do not disturb me for any reason at all. If anyone even knocks on my door, you're fired." He hung up and tossed the phone onto the floor without caring about where it landed. "No one will bother us now. Alvin can be trusted to guard that door with his life." He grabbed the back of Proctor's head hard and shoved his tongue into Proctor's mouth.

They kissed this way for a few minutes, until Proctor was on his back and Blair had three fingers up Proctor's ass as deeply as they would go. Proctor hadn't made out with a man this way in years. Blair continued to probe him for a few more minutes, then removed his fingers and told Proctor to take off his shoes, socks, and pants. Proctor couldn't resist no matter how hard he tried. He didn't only want the sex for the sake of getting off. He wanted to be close to Blair and to experience everything about Blair one more time. He would have settled for just a hug and a kiss if that was all Blair had wanted to do.

Blair, however, seemed as excited and eager as he always did. He pulled a condom out of his pocket and pulled down his zipper. He pulled his dick out of his suit pants and covered it. When Proctor was naked from the waist down, Blair slid up on the sofa behind Proctor and wrapped his arms around him in a tight bear hug. Blair held him tightly and they kissed. He started bucking his hips slowly and this time his dick found Proctor's hole without needing any guidance at all. The head entered Proctor all by itself, and the rest followed until Blair was inside as far as he could go.

They were both on their sides, facing the office door. When Blair began to bite Proctor's neck and fuck at the same time, Proctor hoped no one would come in and find them in this position. Poor Alvin Schlock; if he caught them like this he'd either run out screaming with his arms in the air or stand there with his tongue hanging. It started out slowly, with Blair and Proctor on their sides and Blair fucking, biting, and kissing very slowly. In this spoon position, Blair was able to gain momentum and move at a much faster pace. In no time at all, Proctor's left leg went up and he pointed his toes. Proctor hadn't been fucked sideways in a long time either. He'd forgotten about how stimulated he could become in this position—all he had to do was lie there and lift his leg to feel the beginnings of his climax. It seemed to be working out well for Blair, too. He slid all the way in and all the way out without missing a single beat. The only sounds that came from him were the occasional suction noises from between Proctor's legs and light, soft moans.

By the time they were ready to climax, Blair had lifted Proctor's white shirt all the way up to his chest and he was squeezing Proctor's chest muscles so hard his fingers burned against Proctor's skin. But that only made it better. The harder he squeezed Proctor's chest, the higher Proctor's leg went up.

At one point, as Proctor reached down to jack, Blair plunged into him so hard the top of Proctor's head hit the sofa arm. Proctor jacked faster, his left leg went higher, and his right went dead straight against the sofa cushions. He knew he couldn't moan or yell out loud; he bit his lip so he wouldn't squeal. Blair started bucking faster and squeezing Proctor's chest harder. A second later, Blair grunted softly and climaxed. A second after that, Proctor sprayed the glass coffee table while Blair sucked on the back of his neck.

When Proctor lowered his left leg, he rested it on Blair's left thigh and relaxed all his muscles. Then he reached down between his legs with his left hand and rubbed his fingers around the part of Blair's shaft that was shoved into his hole.

Blair kissed him and said, "What are you doing?" He was still holding Proctor's chest muscles and squeezing them gently.

Proctor smiled and said, "I just wanted to actually touch you while you were inside me. I'm amazed that something so big and thick can actually get into my body this way. And, that it can feel so damn good, too. I didn't feel any pain that time, not even at first." He ran his index finger around the place where the lips of his anus were clamped around Blair's shaft.

Blair laughed. "I'm not that big."

Proctor didn't reply to this. It was true, indeed. Blair wasn't that big, nor was he that thick. Proctor had been with bigger men but they hadn't always been wonderful experiences. He knew how to accommodate extra-large men, even when it wasn't the most pleasurable experience. But with Blair it had never been anything but wonderful. While it wasn't fireworks and explosions, it was a series of sparks and sensations that made him feel a sense of gratitude more than anything else. Though Blair's cock wasn't the biggest or thickest compared to other men, it was bigger than Proctor's anus and this was the part Proctor found amazing. Anything that large and thick being forced into something so small and tight should have hurt; it should have made Proctor writhe in pain. With some guys, Proctor had been in pain and he couldn't wait for the sex to end. Yet with Blair it fit so well and made Proctor feel so complete, all he wanted to do was spread his legs and hold it inside his body for as long as he could.

And that was what he wanted to do that day. "Don't pull out yet."

"I have to," Blair said.

"Why?"

"Because we have to figure out where those paintings are located, so we can solve this case."

Chapter Eleven

For a man like Proctor, the simple act of being desired was often more important than the act of sex. If he'd been born in an earlier time, a long courtship would have been essential to him. As a model, he'd been in the public eye for most of his adult life and he'd grown accustomed to people complimenting and praising his looks with regard to his work. And though he wanted to think none of this was important in his private life, or that he needed this kind of attention when he wasn't working, there was a small part of him that craved the superficial attention just as much in private as he did in public. He'd never wanted to be one of those obsessive celebrities who let their work define them. But it would have been virtually impossible to split himself into two different people.

Blair Huntingdon not only gave him the attention he craved out loud, Blair did it silently, too. He would glance at Proctor without even realizing what he was doing and stare at his legs or his ass. Sometimes he'd rub his jaw and whistle back. Other times he'd lick his lips and make fists. Once, when Proctor bent over to fix his pant leg, he caught Blair staring at his ass and making subtle fuck motions with his pelvis. Though Proctor never called this to Blair's attention, he noticed it on occasion and kept it to himself. It made him smile to think that someone on this Earth cared that much about him, even if it was someone like Blair, who could be extremely pushy and annoying.

After they fucked on the leather sofa, Blair pulled out and removed the condom. He stood up, shoved his dick back into his pants, and walked around the desk so he could throw the condom into a trash can next to his chair. He told Proctor to put on his pants and get dressed. He said he wanted to call Alvin Schlock into the office and ask him a few questions. When Proctor asked why he wanted to talk to Alvin, Blair smiled and said, "I just remembered he said he was a pilot when I hired him."

Proctor zipped up his pants and reached down for his socks and shoes. "That funny little guy is a pilot?" He didn't look like he knew how to ride a bike, let alone fly a plane.

"That's what he told me when I hired him," said Blair. "He told me he stopped flying after he developed an intense fear of flying. He said it happened overnight. That's one reason why I hired him. I'm drawn to complicated people." He winked at Proctor, and then he pressed the intercom and asked Alvin to step into the office.

When Alvin poked his bushy brown head through the cracked door, Proctor was still putting on his shoes and socks. Alvin sent Proctor a naughty smile, as if he knew what they'd just done, then glanced down at the floor and said, "You wanted to see me, Mr. Huntingdon?"

"C'mon in, Alvin," Blair said, with a lighter, carefree tone. "I'd like to ask you a few questions about flying." Whenever he spoke with Alvin, he seemed to use a more encouraging, nurturing tone than he did with other people.

While Blair showed Alvin the numbers on the bottom of the ring, Proctor finished putting on his shoes. When he stood up and walked to the desk, they were searching for something on the computer and Proctor didn't have a clue about what they were discussing. It sounded too mathematical and complicated to worry about. It was the kind of thing that could give Proctor a headache that would last the rest of the day. So he sat down in a chair opposite the desk and listened as if he were hanging on every word they said, pretending to be interested. He was really watching the way Blair's dick moved around in his suit pants when he leaned over. When he moved to the right, his dick went up slightly and Proctor could see the outline of the head. If Blair ever discovered Proctor was looking at him this way, Blair would never let him live it down.

About a half an hour later, right after Alvin and Blair came up with something Blair seemed to find interesting, Alvin went back out front and shut the office door. When they were alone, Blair smiled at Proctor and said, "I think we have an address now, and it's not too far from here, believe it or not. The secret to the lost Pierre Bouvier paintings have been right under our noses the whole time. I'm not surprised. Those Calvin guys would have wanted to be near this information."

"I don't understand," Proctor said. "If Dwayne, his father, and the grandfather had these paintings so close to home, then why didn't they ever cash in on them? It doesn't make sense."

Blair stood up and put on his suit jacket. "They were probably terrified for their lives all these years," he said. "Evidently, they had good reason. We're talking about millions of dollars' worth of famous art. Remember that Nazi soldier who got stiffed when he came to America expecting to find the paintings? The soldier the grandfather was supposed to be holding the paintings for until he came here?"

"Yes."

"Well, I'll bet anything he spent his life trying to find them, and that he now has family who has been looking for these paintings, too. Greed is an interesting thing. Some people will center their lives on it. And we're talking about big bucks here."

Proctor thought about this for a moment. He stood up and said, "So this means we're still in as much danger as we were when those two thugs came into my house?"

Blair shrugged. "I'm afraid we're probably in danger now more than ever."

"What do we do? Go to the police with this information? Maybe we should let them solve the case. It'll be safer."

Blair grabbed his keys from his desk and said, "Hell, no. Why should the cops get all the credit after we've done all the hard work? I want the agency to get credit for this. We're going on the hunt for some hidden paintings today in downtown L.A. Let's roll, baby."

Proctor followed him out of the office and down the hall. In the garage, they climbed into a dark gray sedan Blair had rented after they found the dead guy in the back of the BMW. Blair drove onto Wilshire Boulevard. Proctor read from a set of directions that Alvin Schlock had written out for Blair.

It turned out to be an address in downtown Los Angeles, surrounded by high rises, not far from the tallest building in the United States west of the Mississippi. They parked in an indoor garage and walked into the lobby of the building owned and run by the Buffalo United Insurance Company. In the main lobby, there was a huge bronze statue of a buffalo just like the one on the ring.

Blair glanced at the buffalo and smiled. "Does that look familiar?"

"It's like the one on the ring."

"Exactly."

Proctor glanced back and forth with his hands in his pockets. "But how do we know where to look now? This place is huge." It seemed so pointless.

Blair shrugged. "I have a feeling this is the building where Dwayne and his father and grandfather worked all their lives. I remember Dwayne's boyfriend mentioning it. At the time, I didn't take think it was important. If the information beneath the ring is all in code, there were three numbers that had nothing to do with the address. They are the numbers 36, 42, and 51, and they have nothing to do with the actual location. They appear to be meaningless, at a glance."

"So what does it *mean*?" This was all going right over Proctor's head.

"If I'm correct, and I'm hoping I am, this building probably has fifty stories and we have to go up to the roof. I don't think it has 42 or 36. It seems taller."

So they crossed to one of the express elevators and stepped inside just as the doors were opening. There were two other men in business suits with them and they couldn't speak. But when Blair looked down and pressed a button for the fiftieth floor, he glanced up at Proctor and sent him a quick smile. Proctor took a deep breath and exhaled. This has to be more than a coincidence.

The two men got off several floors below the fiftieth floor. Blair and Proctor rode to the top floor in silence. When they stepped out, Blair seemed to know exactly where he was going. He told Proctor he'd worked in the maintenance department in a building just like this while he'd been in college. He said they were all the same and he knew how to find a door that would lead them to the roof without any problem. He also knew how to avoid being spotted by security cameras so no one in security would know they were up there.

Proctor followed him and did what he was told, sliding against walls, slithering around corners, without asking any questions this time. Before Proctor knew it, they were climbing a flight of metal steps that led them out onto the flat roof of what seemed like the top of the world. Proctor walked into the warm sunshine and spread his arms apart. "Isn't it wonderful up here?"

Blair sent him a look and rubbed his stomach. "If you say so. I'd rather be down on the first floor. I'm not too fond of heights."

This was interesting. Proctor had considered Blair absolutely fearless up until now. "It's not that bad," he said. "Besides, we're safe up here. There's a three-foot rail around the roof top. It's like a private, secret world up here." He laughed and walked to the edge of the roof and glanced down at the street. The people looked like ants, and the cars reminded him of little cigarettes. He hadn't felt this exhilarated in ages. "We're safe unless we get too close to the edge or the rail."

Blair covered his eyes with one hand and reached forward with the other. "Stop that, you idiot. Get over here right now before you fall off and kill yourself. Just watching you stand that close to the edge made my nuts pop up in my sack."

Proctor laughed again and took another step toward the edge. "It's perfectly safe. I love heights. It makes me feel invincible."

"Yeah, well, get your pretty little invincible ass over here and help me figure out where these paintings could be stashed. Because I don't have a clue about what to do now."

Though Proctor was enjoying the view, he decided not to upset Blair. He could see Blair was visibly shaken by the way his skin had turned a pale shade of gray. So he walked back to the door and glanced at the directions Alvin had written down. Then he tapped his chin and said, "It has to be something symbolic. Something that would tie things together. Maybe the other numbers, 42 and 36, are clues."

"I know," Blair said. "But what?"

"Let me think," Proctor said. Although Proctor had never been technical or mathematical, he was good with more creative, emotional problem solving. He had good intuitive instincts, and he'd always been told by his friends he was one of the most empathetic people on the planet.

He looked sideways, across the long, narrow flat section where they stood, to see if there was anything even remotely symbolic to a hidden art collection. For that matter, where on Earth would anyone be able to store a hidden art collection in such a dangerous place? He glanced at the number again and looked up.

That was when it hit him with a jolt. High above their heads, at the very top of this building, there was a solid bronze buffalo with a thin bronze ring around it. This part of the building was simply decoration; the buffalo was the insurance company logo. Though the buffalo wasn't identical to the cheap ring with the engraving, it was very close.

Proctor pointed up and said, "Look up there. I'll bet there's something up there. Maybe there's a hidden compartment near the buffalo where the art work was stored all these years. Maybe there's a hidden doorway leading to a closet or something. The Calvin guys worked in maintenance here and they probably knew every single inch of this building."

Blair pulled the ring out of his pocket. He glanced the buffalo on the ring, then up at the buffalo on the building inside the thin gold ring. "That's awfully far-fetched. I guess it might be connected."

Proctor slapped him on the back. "Of course it's connected. A buffalo *on* a ring, and now there's a buffalo *in* a ring up there on the building. The only slight difference is that the buffalo on the cheap ring is on a plain. The buffalo attached to the building isn't on a plain. He's just standing there."

"But how do we get up there?" Blair asked. He had his hand against his stomach.

"It looks like it's easy to get up there." There was a long wall of intricate design that led upward from the roof deck to the buffalo design. From a distance, it looked like swirls and scrollwork to provide superficial architectural design to what would have been an otherwise bland, beige concrete building. Up close, the scrolls were set about two feet apart, resembling a ladder that would lead up to the buffalo logo attached to the building.

When Blair heard this, he put the ring back into his pocket and gently moved Proctor to the side. "I'll go up and check it out."

"You're terrified of heights," Proctor said. "I'll go. I don't have a problem with heights. I like heights. The higher I am, the better I feel."

"You're crazy," Blair said. "I'm going up. This is one of those times when the dominant top guy has to take control. You just stand back there and look pretty."

Oh, how Proctor hated it when men like Blair said things like this to him. Just because Proctor preferred to be on the receiving end during sex, didn't mean he wasn't every bit of the man Blair was. He saw the way Blair's hands were shaking and he didn't want Blair to hurt himself. He didn't want to bruise Blair's inflated ego either. So he conceded, in a low voice, and said, "Maybe you should let me. I have experience in mountain climbing." He had been mountain climbing before and he'd loved it. He wasn't a pro. But he knew how to hold on without shaking.

Blair grabbed one of the scrolls and heaved forward. "I'm good," he said. "This is nothing."

But when he tried to climb up another step, he slipped on the scroll, lost his grip, and tumbled down. He landed about an inch from the edge of the roof, with his head hanging over the rail. When he looked down, his face turned bright red and he jumped up to his feet so fast his hair flew sideways.

"Let me," Proctor said.

Blair refused to listen. "I'm fine," he said. "I have to get a better grip, is all."

After about five more tries without success, Blair finally stepped aside and let Proctor have his turn. Blair frowned and said, "Be my guest."

Proctor said, "Thank you," then proceeded to remove his shoes, socks, and pants.

"I hate to say this," Blair said, "I never thought I would say this either. But I don't think this is the time or the place for a quick fuck, baby, no matter how tempting it is. Keep your pants on."

"Try not to think with a filthy mind all the time," Proctor said. He pulled off his pants and handed them to Blair. "I can't climb in these tight jeans. I can't spread my legs wide enough. And I can get better footing in my bare feet that I can in expensive leather boots." He'd worn a long white dress shirt that day over his jeans. The tails came down to the middle of his thighs and he wasn't exposed with his pants off. He'd worn swimsuits that showed more of his body than this.

Blair leered at his naked legs and grabbed his dick. He smiled and said, "I just hope no one on the street looks up and sees this, because if they do, there's going to be a pileup down there on the street."

Proctor ignored him and turned toward the building. When he started climbing, he stepped from one scroll to the next effortlessly. The height didn't bother him. The scrolls weren't too bad on his feet. The only slight discomfort was that it wasn't easy to grip the top of the scrolls with his palms.

As he climbed, Blair stood below and watched. "Don't worry, baby. I'm not looking up our shirt. I can't see your ass. Neither can that pigeon that just flew into the wall."

Proctor glanced down at him and smirked. Blair had the driest sense of humor. Though Proctor never would have admitted this to Blair, he liked being up this high, naked from the waist down, above most of Los Angeles. He even started to get an erection halfway to the top.

When he reached the top, he had to cross sideways from the scroll work, step on to a narrow shelf, and grab the buffalo's tail for support.

"There's a small opening behind the buffalo's tail," he said. "I think I see something in there. I'm going to step over and reach inside."

"Be careful," Blair said. "My nuts are in my throat now watching you up there."

It didn't look like a difficult step to take. But when he reached for the buffalo's tail with both hands and hopped on the narrow shelf, the tail broke loose from the top part of the buffalo's ass and Proctor missed the narrow shelf. A small black bag flew out of the opening behind the tail and Proctor wound up dangling in mid-air, swinging back. He still had the roof deck below him. But even that fall could have done serious harm. When he glanced up, he saw the only thing keeping him in place was a thin piece of the buffalo's tail that was still attached to the bottom part of the buffalo's ass.

But more than that, the white dress shirt rode up to the middle of Proctor's waist and he felt a cool breeze. "Help me, Blair. Do something. I'm going to fall. And I'm naked from the waist down. If I don't die or wind up with two broken legs, I'll wind up going to jail for this."

"I'll be right back," Blair said. "Just hang on. You'll be fine. I'll save you."

"Don't leave me here," Proctor said. This was definitely a good reason to start wearing underwear more often.

"I'll be right back," Blair said.

By the time Blair returned, Proctor had managed to hoist his body up so he could loop his right leg around the buffalo's tail. Though part of the tail had separated from the building, it wasn't as bad as he'd thought it was. The rest of the buffalo's tail was actually pretty sturdy, at least the piece that was still attached to the buffalo's ass. He knew he'd be safe as long as he didn't make any sudden moves. After he wrapped his leg around the tail, he managed to straddle the tail, get into a seated position, and pull his shirt down. The only problem was the bottom of the thick round tail was wedged up in his ass crack. The goddamn buffalo's tail was cold and it sent a chill up his ass, through his spine, and stopped at the top of his head. This was another good reason to wear underwear.

"I'm back," Blair said, carrying a long aluminum ladder. "I'll get you down."

He turned the ladder and rested it against the building. The top of the ladder met the bottom of the buffalo's tail with about a foot to spare. Blair looked up and said, "Now, come down very slowly and concentrate. And whatever you do, don't look down."

Proctor rolled his eyes. He lowered his left foot to the ladder and slowly pulled his right leg off the buffalo's tail. "Just shut up and hold the ladder still," he said. "I can look down and I'll be fine. I'm not afraid of heights, idiot. I'm just afraid the dude holding the ladder is going to let go."

When he reached the fourth rung down, the ladder started to wobble. Then it slowly pulled away from the wall and started leaning over the street. Proctor screamed and said, "What the fuck is happening down there? I told you to hold the goddamn ladder still."

"I'm trying," Blair said. "It's not as easy as you think. I can't get the right angle because there's not enough room to step back."

Proctor glanced down and he saw Blair struggling with the ladder. He knew the ladder was about to tip forward at any moment, so he grabbed a rung and held it as tightly as he could. A moment after that, the ladder tipped forward and Proctor went down with it. It fell like one long, thin plank of wood. One end of the ladder ended up suspended over the railing that bordered the rooftop and the other wound up stuck beneath an indentation in the building. It was a good thing there was an indentation there, because if there hadn't, been there would have been no way Blair would have been able to hold the ladder much longer. It still wasn't exactly a perfect situation, not by any means. Blair found himself dangling over the street, holding the rung with both hands, with his shirt up above his waist again.

"The ladder is secure," Blair said. "It's wedged into the wall. All you have to do is climb back here, rung by rung."

"I can't believe this," Proctor shouted. "I'm suspended in midair, half naked, for all of L.A. to see. I swear if this winds up in the tabloids, I'm going to cut your balls off, Blair."

"What did I do?" Blair asked. "I'm wearing underwear today."

"You were supposed to hold the fucking ladder still," Proctor said.

"Let's argue later," Blair said. "We'll have cake. Right now, just grab the next rung and started moving toward me very slowly. You'll be fine. Just don't look down."

Proctor reached forward and grabbed the next rung. He jerked his entire body and moved one rung closer to the building. "If you tell me not to look down one more time, I'm going to jump to my death on purpose."

"Okay," Blair said. "Calm down. Concentrate on getting back here. Look down all you want."

When he started to swing back and forth and he realized the magnitude of what was happening, Proctor felt a wave of panic rush through his entire body. His heart began to race, he couldn't move his arms, and he started screaming.

"What's wrong?"

"I can't move," Proctor said. "I shouldn't have looked down. I'm going to fall. I don't think I can hang on much longer. I'm frozen."

"Hold on. I'm coming out there."

"But you're afraid of heights," Proctor said. He looked down. When he saw the cars passing on the street, he started to scream again.

While Proctor was screaming, Blair must have found the courage deep down inside and tossed his fear of heights aside. He somehow managed to climb out to the middle of the ladder, as it dangled fifty one stories over the street, and reached for Proctor's hands. But he grabbed Proctor's shirt by accident and pulled too hard. The shirt ripped up the sides, split down the back, and half of it went flying down to the street. Then Blair reached down and grabbed Proctor's arm. He held the ladder for support with his right hand and yanked Proctor up to the flat side of the ladder with his left.

When he knew it was safe, Proctor lifted his leg and threw it over Blair's body. He grabbed the sides of the ladder with both hands and rested his torso flat against the rungs. As he was about to take a deep breath, he felt something warm and wet on the bottom of his ass. He glanced back and saw Blair licking it.

"*Are you crazy?*" he said.

Blair smiled. "It was in my face. I couldn't help it."

"What do we do now? I don't want to freeze up again." He was afraid he might panic and he wouldn't be able to move. With the ladder suspended this way, even though he could see through the rungs, he felt as if he were holding a plank and it gave him a false sense of security as long as he didn't move at all.

"You turn around, climb over me, and I'll follow you. We'll crawl back to the roof very slowly."

"I'm not sure I can do this. I'm afraid to move."

"You'll be fine. Just move very slowly and concentrate."

When they were both finally back on the roof, Proctor fell into Blair's arms and they remained that way in silence for a moment. Then Blair kissed him and stepped back. He removed his suit jacket and helped

Proctor put his arms through the sleeves. The shirt had ripped in a way that exposed most of Proctor's naked back. Blair kissed him again and said, "I don't want you catching cold or anything."

Proctor smiled and buttoned the jacket. "You're braver than I thought you were. You can be very sweet sometimes."

Blair shrugged. "I saw a few planes pass by and I figured I'd better cover you up. I don't want any mid-air collisions either."

Then Proctor glanced down at the rooftop floor and pointed to the black bag that had fallen out of the hole near the buffalo's tail. "Look, that might be something important. That's what was in the hole behind the buffalo's tail."

Blair picked it up and opened the black bag. He pulled out a set of keys attached to a key chain. On the key chain, he saw the name, address, and phone number of a storage facility in Los Angeles. Below the phone number it said, "Unit 16." He dangled the keys in Proctor's face and said, "I have a feeling we've found the lost art of Pierre Bouvier."

"So the art wasn't hidden up there," Proctor said.

"Of course not. That would have been too easy. These guys wanted to make sure it was almost impossible to find."

Before Proctor could reply, a voice came from the other end of the roof and they both turned. There was an older man in a tweed sport jacket pointing a gun at them. He looked familiar. Proctor thought for a moment, then remembered him as the older man who had been in the restaurant lobby when Rolf Braun had shoved the ring on Proctor's fingers. It was the same man Proctor had seen briefly in the jewelry store.

"Hand everything over to me," the old man said. He spoke with a slight accent that could have been German. But it wasn't strong enough to be full German.

Proctor moaned. "You might have to give it to him. I think this guy has been following us for a while now and he's not joking around. I saw him the night Rolf Braun died in the restaurant."

Proctor and Blair exchanged a quick glance. Blair tossed the keys into the black bag and threw the bag at Proctor. Then Blair climbed onto the ladder and back out over the street. He sat down on the ladder between two rungs, with his legs dangling over the sides, facing the building.

The old man with the gun moved closer. Proctor glanced down at the black bag and then up at Blair. "What should I do?"

Blair said, "Toss me the bag now."

Proctor threw the bag and Blair caught it.

Blair smiled at the old man and said, "If you want it, you old fucker, you've got to come out here and get it from me."

Proctor didn't see that happening anytime soon.

But the old man growled and said, "Fuck you." He pointed the gun at Proctor for a moment, then shoved it back into his tweed jacket. He lifted his leg and climbed on the ladder very slowly. Though his hands were shaking, likely more from old age than fear, he had a determined look. "You thought I wouldn't do this. Fuck you. There's nothing I wouldn't do to get that bag. Nothing in the world. You'll be sorry you fucked around with me. I've been trying to get that information for many years. My father was a proud German officer who trusted those fucking liars with the paintings. I've been looking for them all my life."

The old man was too heavy. The extra weight caused the thin aluminum ladder to start bending where it rested against the rail that surrounded the rooftop.

"Go back," Blair said. "The ladder's not going to hold up."

Proctor glanced down at the ladder. There was nothing he could do.

The old man held the ladder tighter and he continued to glare at Blair with a desperate expression. For a moment, it looked as if he might go back. But he started moving forward and the ladder continued to bend downward. When he reached Blair, and the two men were eye to eye, the old man lunged for the black bag and the ladder went down fast. Blair held the ladder rung with one hand and the bag with the other. The old man flipped over Blair's head, caught hold of Blair's hand, and wound up dangling beneath Blair well below the last rung on the ladder. The old man's hands slipped until he was holding nothing but the black bag as tightly as he could. The only thing between him and fifty one stories was a flimsy piece of fabric that contained a set of keys to a storage unit.

Proctor glanced down with wide eyes and his fingertips pressed to his cheeks. The old guy held on to the bag for a long time, as Blair tried his best to lift the old guy to safety. But the black bag eventually ripped from the pressure and the keys fell out and flew to the ground. When the old man saw the keys fall, a despondent look fell across his face and he looked down to see where they went. Falling from that height, the keys could have landed anywhere. They disappeared instantly. After that, it was as if the old guy stopped fighting on purpose. A minute after he saw the keys fall out of the bag, he released his grip and fell 51 stories to his death.

While this had been going on, Proctor had been staring at the ladder, hoping it wouldn't break completely. He heard sirens in the distance coming in their direction. He knew Blair was hanging on by a thin source. The ladder was ready to split from the rail at any moment and there was nothing he could do except pray that Blair had the stamina to climb to safety.

Chapter Twelve

It took the next three days to sort the case out with the police and the French authorities. Though no one ever found the keys that fell out of the black bag, Blair did remember the storage unit number and he led the police to the storage facility with a court order to expose the contents. It had been leased in Dwayne Calvin's name. Before that, the records showed it had been leased in Dwayne's father's name. If Blair and Proctor hadn't shown up when they did, the contents would have been auctioned off eventually now that Dwayne Calvin was dead. Dwayne hadn't expected to die so young, and so accidentally.

When the police opened the storage unit door, everyone stood back and held their breath. But that wasn't the end, not by any means. The lost art wasn't there; the storage unit contained nothing but old furniture and junk from the 1940s. Blair said he expected this. It would have been too simple for them to hide the art there, and far too dangerous. It was just another sneaky trick created by the Calvin men to throw off the enemy. Proctor wasn't sure they would ever find it now.

With the police, Blair and Proctor searched the storage unit from top to bottom. This wasn't normal protocol, but Blair knew one of the officers and the police looked the other way. Blair eventually found another clue inside a rock maple dresser shoved into the back of the storage unit behind an old dress form that no one else would have noticed. This time the clue was a worthless wristwatch with a broken band and a bent second hand. It didn't even tell time. But it had more numbers engraved on the back that didn't seem to make sense, including the numbers 36 and 42, which Blair seemed to think were somehow connected to the numbers on the ring.

The watch had been wrapped in a small piece of fabric that had small buffalo images everywhere. This stumped them all for a while. Proctor thought about it so hard his head began to hurt. The police wanted to call in experts; they weren't even certain the watch had a connection to the lost art. Proctor agreed with them. He didn't want to waste time. But Blair insisted there had to be a connection and that he could figure the engraving out if they gave him a few hours alone with a computer. He literally begged. Though Proctor wasn't sure how he did it, Blair finally figured out a way to add up all the numbers on the engraving and came up with an address that matched the exact physical street address of the Buffalo United Insurance Company. When the police saw this, and Blair explained it to them, they agreed it was more than a coincidence.

They wound up back in the Buffalo United Insurance Company building downtown. They searched the entire building until they found a secluded rear wall in the basement with a small buffalo engraving. Blair spotted the engraving first, as if he knew exactly what he'd been looking for all along. Proctor and the police officers had to walk up and stare for a moment to see it was a buffalo. At a glance, it looked more like a smudge. But the wall turned out to be a secret door that led to a hidden room.

When they entered the hidden room, they finally found the lost paintings of Pierre Bouvier that had been missing since World War II. Evidently, this is why the Calvin men had always remained so close to this building, including Dwayne who'd only worked there part time. The hidden room was dry, almost airtight. The cool basement had kept the paintings intact all these years. Although some would need minor restoration, most were in very good shape and had been cared for very well.

Proctor and Blair had no idea the French government had been quietly searching for the paintings all those years, nor did they know there was a $1,000,000 reward being offered to the person who found them and returned them. Proctor and Blair received full credit for recovering the paintings. They donated $100,000 to the city of Los Angeles for new police cars, and were allowed to keep the rest. Blair said this reward money would be plenty to give The Rainbow Private Detective Agency a jump start to a new beginning.

The only problem was Proctor wasn't certain he wanted to move forward in this direction. He'd never been so terrified in his life, especially being surrounded by so many dead people. His detective skills were lacking, too. If it hadn't been for Blair's instincts and knowledge, Proctor would never have found the paintings on his own. He had tentative plans to restart his own career as a model, with hopes of hitting it really big just one more time the same way he'd hit it big with the wet swim suit poster. But he also knew, deep down, luck had played a huge part in his success, not to mention youth. He wasn't in his twenties anymore, and he never would be again.

When news about the lost art of Pierre Bouvier broke, and when the world discovered the extent to which Pierre Bouvier had been brutally persecuted for being openly homosexual during World War II by the Nazis, it went viral. The timing couldn't have been more perfect. There had been a media event about gays in the military a week earlier. The name Proctor Gamble made every major headline from large print newspapers to small time Internet blogs. The headlines always read along the same lines: "Former Male Model Turns Gay Private Detective." Proctor's agent called and said there were so many offers to do news interviews and talk shows he didn't know where to start. The world seemed just as interested in the fact that two gay men like Proctor and Blair had solved the case of the missing paintings as they were in knowing more about Proctor's huge life change to become a private detective.

For once, being openly gay helped. The world seemed fascinated by this, probably because Proctor didn't fit the typical mold of a private detective; neither did Blair. It was the best publicity Proctor had ever had in his entire career. They were both heroes. The only thing that might have worked out better would have been if he'd signed to do a bridal show on the gay TV network, or a talk show on Oprah's new network. Best of all, the publicity from all this had been free this time. He'd paid public relations firms small fortunes over the years to garner the kind of publicity he'd received with this lost art case in only a couple of nights.

When things finally settled down, Blair drove Proctor back to his home in the Hollywood Hills. He'd been sleeping in the office every night. They been so busy wrapping up the case with the police that Proctor hadn't had a decent night's sleep in days. The only thing he wanted to do was fall into bed and shut his eyes. After that, he wanted to get Constance back from the vet and hold her in his arms.

But Blair insisted on walking him to the front door. Then he insisted on opening the door for him and walking him into the front hall. Before Proctor knew what was happening, Blair's hand was down the back of his pants and they were upstairs in Proctor's bedroom.

"I think you should leave," Proctor said. "My head is still spinning. I'm not used to all this drama. I need quiet time now."

Blair removed his jacket and threw it on the floor. He grabbed Proctor and pulled him closer. "I want you."

Proctor smiled and tried to push him away. But when their lips met and their tongues locked, he fell backward on the bed and spread his legs. "I should chase you out of here with a baseball bat," Proctor said, as Blair stood up to remove the rest of his clothes.

Blair smiled and removed his shoes and socks. He threw them over his shoulder like a slob, then pulled down his pants. "You loved every minute of it," he said, sending Proctor a coy smile. "You never had more fun in your life. And you know it."

Though Proctor had been terrified, he couldn't argue this point. He'd never felt so exhilarated and eager for more. All his life and as a model, he'd gone to work and he'd done what he was expected to do—which was mostly standing around and smiling. For the first time, he felt challenged and worthy of something. He wasn't sure exactly what that was yet, but it felt good anyway.

Blair removed his shirt and put on a condom. He stood over the end of the bed, where Proctor was flat on his back, and spread his legs. He leaned back, grabbed his erection, and shook it slowly. He smiled and asked, "Do you still want me to leave now that you've seen this big boy?"

Proctor laughed. He had never met a man with such a huge ego and a sense of humor. He smirked and rolled his eyes. "Yes. You should put that thing away, go back to wherever it is you live, and let me get some sleep. I'll be in a much better mood in the morning. We can talk more than."

"Take off your pants," Blair said in a low, firm tone. He wasn't ready to leave.

"No."

"If you don't, I'll take them off for you."

As Proctor opened his mouth to reply, Blair climbed on top of him and he grabbed the back of his neck. When Blair kissed him, he used his other hand to unfasten Proctor's pants. After that, the kissing became so intense Proctor lost track and wound up naked beneath Blair. And it wasn't because Blair had removed his clothes. All Blair had done was unfasten Proctor's pants. Proctor had removed his own clothes, of his own free will, without a protest. So many people seemed to get so upset by fake rape scenes these days that he didn't want to chance it. He'd once done a shoot for a high-end clothing designer where the final images suggested a hint of rape or brute force. It wasn't anything Proctor considered serious. It wasn't real. Proctor never would have laughed at something as serious as an actual rape. But that ad brought out every nutty loon in the universe and he never thought the nasty e-mails would stop.

This time they did something different, but not until the end. It was something Proctor knew Blair would like, but might not have the nerve to ask for. When he was naked, Blair hoisted Proctor up to the middle of the bed and crawled between his legs. Proctor spread his legs, lifted them, and Blair mounted him as quickly as he usually did. While Blair slid in and out of his body, Proctor kissed him and caressed his neck and shoulders and head. He moaned in hushed tones to let Blair know he wanted more and he didn't care how aggressive Blair became. At one point, with Blair deep inside, Proctor's knees wound up pinned to his shoulders. A few minutes after that, his legs wound up over Blair's shoulders while Blair slammed him so hard his head fell off the side of the bed.

This time it didn't seem as though Blair wanted to stop fucking. Each time before this had been fast and calculated. They'd been fighting a clock, trying to get as much passion into a single session as they could. Now, Blair seemed to be doing all the things he'd wanted to do since they first met.

After Blair fucked him on his back, he turned Proctor over and banged him on his stomach until his legs bent at the knee and his feet arched. In this position, Blair took complete control. It really felt like men fucking men in the most classic sense, without hang-ups, inhibitions, and quasi emotional drama. Blair's thrusts went deep and fast, with loud cracks. He seemed to grow harder and thicker with each entry. With his face in a pillow, Proctor let out soft moans and whispers, begging him to go deeper and harder. He reached back with both hands at certain points and grabbed Blair's slim hips as if he were trying to push Blair in even deeper than he already was. Of course, this was impossible. Proctor knew Blair couldn't get into his body any deeper. But he couldn't fight the urge to try anyway.

When Blair was finished fucking Proctor on his stomach, he turned him on his side and lifted his left leg. Blair remained up on his knees, poking Proctor's hole, gazing down at what he was doing the entire time.

When he finished fucking Proctor on his side, he turned him around again and fucked him doggie style. Proctor thought he knew what to expect in this position: it was the way most guys preferred to fuck him. He spread his legs, arched his back, and braced his palms on the bed so his ass would be higher than his head. He never expected Blair to yank him by the waist, lift the lower half of his body up off the bed, and fuck him with his legs dangling in mid-air. For a minute or two, Proctor felt like one of those creepy blow-up dolls, without no control whatsoever. Blair wasn't actually fucking *him*. Blair was ramming Proctor's ass into *his* dick and he wasn't even moving his hips. It grew so intense Proctor had to focus on prolonging his climax so he wouldn't come too soon.

In between these various positions, each time Blair stopped moving, he made sure he kissed Proctor and said something unexpected and absolutely adorable that made Proctor's chest cave in.

After they stopped fucking doggie style, Blair went down on his back and he told Proctor to straddle his dick and ride it for a while. He told him to spread his legs wide and sit all the way down on it. When Proctor did, Blair pulled Proctor's face to his and said, "You're the most beautiful man I've ever met, on the inside and on the outside. You have something that makes me feel like doing wonderful things that I never wanted to do before. I really want to make it work this time."

When Blair said this, Proctor felt a sting in his eyes. No man had ever said things like this to him during sex. He wasn't sure how to reply. So he kissed Blair and spread his legs wider.

Toward the end, Proctor wound up on his back again, with his legs spread and Blair between them. He knew Blair was close to climax. He could tell by the way Blair's eyebrows furrowed and his head kept going backward. Blair started to fuck faster, with that quick, jolting pace he tended to use right before he came. Proctor was close, too. He knew all he had to do was reach down and hold his penis a certain way. But he still wanted to do something different. Something Blair would remember for a long, long time.

While Blair continued to pound him, Proctor held the back of Blair's neck with his left hand and reached between his own legs with his right. He smiled and said, "I want to come first this time, but I want you to hold off for a minute. Can you do that?"

"Oh, baby," Blair said in a desperate tone. "I'm not sure I can. I'm ready to blow a fucking load any second right up your ass."

Proctor smiled. He liked when Blair spoke this way. Jane, his assistant, would have screamed and run out of the bedroom. She might have needed six months of therapy afterward. But not a gay man like Proctor who wanted dick. It was the combination of tender and crude that attracted him *most* to Blair. "Please try. I promise you'll like what I'm going to do to you."

"Okay," Blair said in a wrecked voice. "I'll try not to come."

A moment after that, Proctor lifted his legs, pointed his toes, and exploded. His come went over his head and landed on the wall behind the bed. It was a huge load, too. He glanced back for a second to see it splash against the white wall above the mirrored headboard. He hadn't come in a few days. Hitting the wall wasn't unusual, especially because Blair had been banging him so hard. The vibrations of Blair's dick rubbing against Proctor's prostate would have sent that huge load of come 10 feet more if the goddamn wall hadn't been in the way.

After Proctor came, he didn't waste any time. He lowered his legs. He pushed Blair back. Then he climbed off Blair's dick, off the bed, and went down to the floor on his knees beside the bed. Blair turned and watched him with a stark, confused expression, as not knowing what to expect. Proctor told Blair to turn around and kneel before him at the edge of the bed. When Blair did this, Proctor removed the condom and tossed it over his shoulder. He pressed his palms on Blair's thighs and swallowed Blair's dick until the head hit the back of his throat. It only took a few good sucks and a little pressure from his tongue to get Blair off. Proctor didn't have to use his hands, not one single jerk. Blair's upper body went back and he rested his weight on his palms. When Blair opened his mouth and grunted, he blasted his own huge load of come into Proctor's mouth and said, "Fuck, yes, you dirty little fucker."

Proctor sucked and swallowed without moving his head. His lips were up against Blair's neatly trimmed pubic hairs and his nose rested a few inches below Blair's navel. He didn't slurp, and he didn't make a sound. He didn't gag or make an awkward face. As the come shot out of Blair's dick, he swallowed so gently if anyone had been watching they would have sworn his throat never moved when he swallowed. Blair's come had a sweet flavor. He could have put it on ice cream and licked the bowl clean.

When Blair finally opened his eyes and took a deep breath. He glanced down at Proctor and said, "Damn, baby. You're not only pretty and smart. But you're a lot dirtier than I thought you were." He caressed the top of Proctor's head and smiled. "I like that. No one would ever believe such pretty lips would be capable of doing such dirty, nasty things to a guy."

Proctor continued to suck for a few more minutes. He liked it when a penis either grew hard or soft in his mouth. When he'd drained all there was in Blair's dick tonight, he drew back and climbed into bed. It was late and they were both exhausted. There was no talk about Blair going back to his own place that night. Proctor simply climbed under the covers, rested on his side, and Blair sidled up behind him where they fell into a deep sleep.

At dawn, Proctor surprised Blair with another unforgettable blow job he hadn't planned ahead of time. They both woke up with an intense urge to pee and raced to the bathroom at the same time. But while they were peeing, Proctor reached for Blair's dick and pointed it to the toilet. It grew to a full erection within seconds, so Proctor went down on his knees on the bathroom floor and sucked him off before they even had a chance to flush the toilet. After that, they returned to bed and slept for another three hours. This time Blair woke Proctor by climbing onto his back and mounting him beneath the covers.

By the time they were showered and dressed, they went downstairs and had coffee next to the pool. Proctor turned on his tablet to see what was going on in the world and he did a search for some of the headlines that had been written about the lost art, the gay French artist, and his connection to the case. One headline the day after the story broke read, "Wet Swimsuit Gay Poster Boy Solves Age Old Case." Another one read, "Artist Persecuted For Being Gay Gets Revenge Through Gay Model Proctor Gamble."

Blair glanced at the headlines and lifted his coffee cup. "You're even more famous now than you were before. Money isn't going to be a problem anymore."

"I'm sorry they aren't giving you more credit," Proctor said. He felt bad about the way the media was focusing on him and ignoring Blair. He'd make a small fortune in appearances and interviews alone. He might even get a book deal out of it.

Blair smiled. "It's fine, seriously. I mean that. My goal was to solve the case, return the art to the French government, make a name for the agency, and use your name to do it. I knew what I was doing all along. I don't need attention like that. I just need to know I won."

"We're splitting that reward money right down the middle," Proctor said. "Half goes to you, and the other half goes to me."

Blair set the coffee cup down and sat back. He crossed his legs and smiled. "I was hoping we'd invest the entire reward into the business account and start drawing salaries. My voice mail is loaded with people who want to hire us. I'd like to make my point once again: you need to do this. You're a natural and we'll make this agency the most popular and respected private detective agency in the world."

"I have to think about it," Proctor said. "And I have to think about what's best for my modeling career. Besides, you can do it alone. You don't need me anymore."

That was when Blair's blunt honesty could sting. He leaned forward, reached for Proctor's hands, and squeezed them. "Baby, I think you're gorgeous, but you're not getting any younger. All those guys in the modeling industry are getting younger day by day. You're going to have to face facts sooner or later. Your modeling days are numbered, at best."

Proctor sent him a sharp glance. "Are you saying I'm too old, and that I'm over the hill? I'm only 30." He tended to lie about his age so much he believed it himself sometimes.

Blair smiled. "You're more like 34, 35, but that's beside the point. Even the newspapers are calling you a 'former' model. You have to face facts. And, you have a great career ahead of you as a private detective."

Though Proctor felt a tug in his stomach at the thought of getting older, this wasn't the kind of logic with which he could argue. He knew all too well his modeling days were coming to an end— unless he wanted to wind up modeling dad jeans and plaid shirts in lesser-known catalogues for lower wages. But he wasn't ready to commit to anything yet. "I need time to think it all over."

Blair sighed. He sat back and looked directly into Proctor's eyes. "I just want you to know that I've enjoyed working with you on this case, aside from all the fringe benefits. I'm ready for a partner now. And, I do need you more than you think."

"A *partner?*" Proctor almost choked on his coffee.

"Calm down," Blair said. "I'm not talking about a life partner. I'm talking about a business partner in the agency."

"Ah well," Proctor said. "That's good, because even though we have great sex, getting romantically involved could be dangerous. We're too different. We're too opposite. We'd wind up killing each other. I think we're better suited as fuck buddies."

"But we're great together as detectives," Blair said. "Just say yes. You can have my office. I'll take the smaller one. Or we can share an office if you like. Anything you want, it's yours. You're the boss."

Proctor already knew he was the boss. He set his cup on the table and stood up. "It's too soon. I need time to think. I can't make decisions like this in a hurry."

Blair stood. "Just say yes. You need to do this. I need you to do this. We're great together."

"I need some time alone," he said, as he turned and started walking toward the front door so he could let Blair out.

Blair caught up with him and rested his palm on the small of his back. "How much time?"

"I'm not sure."

"Just give me a hint. Don't leave me hanging. That's not fair."

"Okay, 24 hours," Proctor said. But he only said it to shut him up. Though he wasn't fond of dead bodies and people threatening his life, he couldn't deny this had been one of the most exciting times of his life, without or without the added publicity with or without the great dick he'd been getting. He wasn't ready to sit home and bake yummy cookies, and he wasn't ready to post photos of cute kitty cats on Facebook. He already knew he was going to give the private detective business a shot. He just didn't want Blair to think he was too eager to do this. With a pushy, aggressive man like Blair Huntingdon, appearing too eager about anything would have been a huge mistake. Blair was the kind of man who had to be handled with a quiet passive aggressive approach, so he wouldn't get too cocky and assume complete control. When it came to men like this, Proctor was a master.

When he opened the door for Blair, they were hit with a large group of reporters who had been camped out front since late last night. They were all shouting questions at the same time and it was hard to understand them. They wanted to know about Dwayne Calvin and the old man who fell from the top of the fifty story building. They wanted to know details about the lost art of Pierre Bouvier and how Proctor and Blair had managed to figure out where it was hidden after all these years. Proctor smiled, as he'd been trained to smile in public many years earlier, and Blair stepped in front of him. When Blair started speaking about possible plans for the future, avoiding direct questions, Proctor stood there in silence, listening.

Though running a private detective agency had never been his dream job, there were worse things he could have done with his life. And what he had with Blair, even though he couldn't actually define it yet, was closer to love than anything he'd ever known. Blair felt like family. He had a feeling Blair felt the same way about him. The Rainbow Detective Agency might be the best thing that had happened to him since the wet swim suit poster. While the reporters continued shouting, he experienced the same surge of energy he'd once had when the wet swimsuit poster went viral. At the time, he knew deep down it would be something important. He knew it would change his life.

It was nice to know he could feel that way again.

Excerpt from The Case of The Magic Man
Book Two of The Rainbow Detective Agency

Chapter One

On a cold, rainy night in early April, Alonzo Abertini's shoes rested on the floor beside the bed. His socks sat on the windowsill and his underwear hung from the corner of the television. He'd left his shirt, slacks, and jacket in a heap near the front door because that's where the two guys he'd met at the bar in West Hollywood had removed them. The two guys had left their clothes not far from his. Neither of them had been wearing underwear that night.

Although Alonzo had to admit the two young football players from UCLA surpassed any of the men he'd been with, the low-end hotel in one of L.A.'s less desirable neighborhoods made him feel even more homesick for the hills of Tuscany than he already was. It smelled of damp towels and rancid olive oil. Everything he touched felt thick and fuzzy, as if it hadn't been cleaned in years. The walls were a dismal shade of gray, tarnished with several shades of brown in each corner. The synthetic sheer white drapes had darkened to match the gray walls and the brown industrial carpet made the bottoms of his feet itch. The bed was so lumpy and the pillows so flat Alonzo didn't see how anyone could get a decent night's sleep there.

But he wasn't there for sleep, at least not that night.

Alonzo was in the middle of a 1970s low-slung platform bed with one 21year-old football player on his right and another on his left. All three were on their backs. Alonzo was the only one awake. The one on Alonzo's right, Kyle, had his long hairy calf over Alonzo's smooth leg, and the one on his left, Jarrod, had his muscular thigh over Alonzo's other leg. The two football players had taken turns on Alonzo earlier and now they were napping. Their arms were stretched back above their heads and they looked so peaceful Alonzo couldn't resist reaching down with both hands to gently grope their genitals. From what he could gather, they were a couple in a committed relationship and both were top guys. Every now and then they would cruise the bars looking for a bottom. In jest, they referred to each other as "Toppy" for reasons Alonzo never discovered, and doubled over in laughter each time they did this.

As Alonzo fondled them, he glanced down at Jarrod's armpits and took a quick breath, hoping to inhale his scent without leaning over to disturb him. With his arms all the way back like that, Alonzo could see the way each muscle in the young man's arm was defined. Jarrod was lighter in complexion than Kyle and the hair under his arms had a fuzzy, flaxen appeal that made Alonzo want to lean over and start licking. He glanced over at Kyle's armpits and bit the inside of his mouth. Kyle was darker and tougher and he had the kind of deep football player voice that made Alonzo weak. He knew if he buried his face under Kyle's arm he would close his eyes, inhale, and hold his breath until he went lightheaded.

But Alonzo didn't lick them or sniff them. He didn't do anything but stroke them both very gently, running his fingertips lightly against their scrotums. He didn't want to wake them yet. It would be too soon. He figured he'd let them sleep at least another 20 minutes so they'd be ready to go another round.

In less than a half hour, Alonzo felt both young men growing in his palms. Kyle was longer than Jarrod. But Jarrod was uncircumcised and had the kind of thickness that made a man like Alonzo want to open his legs and arch his back. While he continued to stroke, Kyle opened his legs wider and Jarrod let out a soft moan. As the heavy rain pounded the foggy hotel room window, and the neon sign from the massage parlor across the street flashed in red, Alonzo brought both young men to full erections in no time at all.

When he was hard, Kyle bucked his hips and lowered his arm. He wrapped it around Alonzo's shoulder and kissed him, inserting his tongue. A second or two after that, Jarrod leaned over and slid his tongue into Alonzo's mouth at the same time. While all three tongues melded together, Alonzo tightened his grip and stroked them faster. He didn't have to glance down between his own legs to know he was as erect as they were.

It didn't take long for big, strong Kyle to grab the back of Alonzo's neck and push him forward. Kyle, the more aggressive of the two, had so far always made the first move. Alonzo went forward without a hint of resistance. When his face was between Kyle's hairy legs, he opened his mouth, wrapped his lips around the head of Kyle's dick, and started sucking. He closed his eyes and inhaled the masculine scent. He could still smell a hint of spicy body wash now combined with his natural aroma. He rested his head on Kyle's lower abdomen and his palm on his hairy thigh. While he sucked Kyle off he continued to stroke Jarrod, who was still on his other side, anticipating the exact moment when he would stop sucking Kyle and take a turn between Jarrod's legs. Jarrod seemed to know how much Alonzo liked an uncut dick, and it was probably because of the way Alonzo had chewed and played with his foreskin for so long earlier. While he sucked Kyle, Jarrod reached down and stretched his foreskin out as much as he could to entice Alonzo.

He took turns on them both, sucking until his tongue felt numb. One thing led to another and before Alonzo knew it he was flat on his back and both young men were kneeling over his head. He took turns on them, licking and sucking from their balls all the way to the tips of their dicks. He stroked until he saw pre-come, and then he milked them harder and licked it off with the tip of his tongue while they glanced down at him and stroked his dark wavy hair.

Although they weren't violent in an obvious way, both men were strong—so strong they didn't realize they were hurting Alonzo when they lifted him up and turned him over on his stomach. He didn't wince, and he didn't cry out once. He took the pain, got down on all fours in the middle of the mattress, and spread his legs. He knew what they wanted. While the guys put on condoms, he arched his back and grabbed the sheets. When Kyle mounted him, his head went back and his jaw fell. The thing Alonzo liked most about the way Kyle and Jarrod fucked him was that it wasn't ordinary in the sense that each one didn't spend too much time inside. Alonzo had been fucked by more than one guy before. But this time it was different. Kyle would fuck for a minute or two, and then he would back out and Jarrod would mount him. They would repeat this a minute later. The difference between both men sent sparks shooting through Alonzo's entire body. The way they took turns so fast drove him to distraction. Each time one would pull out and the other would enter, an overwhelming sensation rushed through Alonzo's entire body and brought him closer to the edge.

The second time that night wasn't as long as the first. After about a half hour of taking turns on him, Alonzo knew they were both close when they started repeating the word "fuck" and slapping his ass. They'd done the same thing earlier that night the first time. When they did this, Alonzo knew it was time for him to tighten his sphincter muscle. He knew the friction from this tightness would bring them off faster and make their climaxes more intense. It was such a small gesture on his part, yet it never failed to please the men he was with.

And he knew his technique was working this time with Kyle and Jarrod. They started taking turns less and pounding him with more intensity. Kyle came first. He filled the condom, shouted, "Fuck, man," and slammed into Alonzo so hard he fell forward and landed flat on his stomach. At that exact moment, when his dick rubbed against the old sheets, Alonzo couldn't hold back a minute longer. He came without touching himself from the way Kyle's dick had been rubbing against his prostate.

Kyle fucked for a few more seconds while Jarrod jacked his dick and waited for his turn. Then Kyle pulled out and Jarrod mounted Alonzo while he was still on his stomach. Jarrod took longer than Kyle, which was fine with Alonzo. He had another small climax he hadn't expected. Jarrod pounded Alonzo into the mattress so hard the bed knocked into the old gray plaster wall. When he was finished, he didn't pull out as fast as Kyle. He fell on top of Alonzo and rubbed his sweaty chest against Alonzo's back and said, "Fucking hot, dude." He reached back and slapped Alonzo's ass. "I could line up about 10 more guys next time you're in town."

Alonzo had told both men he was traveling through the United States visiting relatives in different parts of the country. He didn't want anyone to know the real reason why he was in America. This would have been too dangerous. He took a breath and sighed. With an Italian accent that wasn't as thick as it should have been because he consciously worked hard not to have an accent, he said, "I would be more than happy to take care of all your friends."

Kyle had removed the condom by then and tossed it over his shoulder. He leaned over and rubbed his balls in Alonzo's face. He did this often and each time he smiled. "I don't know about that," he said. "I'm starting to think we should just keep you here in America all to ourselves and not tell anyone else about you. Jarrod and I have been looking for a good bottom like you for a long time. We've been together for three years and we've never had this much fun with another guy. Most of the time the other guy prefers one of us over the other. But not you, man. You didn't show an ounce of favoritism."

Alonzo had to think for a moment to process the translation of favoritism in this context. When he understood, he kissed Kyle's balls and said, "That's because I like you guys just the same. There is no favoritism." He laughed. "Maybe we should all live happily ever after together." He'd always dreamed he'd find one man, fall in love, and settle down. But he had to admit the advantages to falling in love with two men, getting fucked by two dicks all the time, and settling down did intrigue him.

Jarrod was still deep inside. He bucked his hips and said, "Seriously, dude. We should think about this. You're the most adorable guy we've met in years. Why don't you think about moving in with us for a while? We can see how it works out. I haven't felt this way about anyone since I met Kyle." He glanced at Kyle and shrugged to see if he approved.

Kyle caressed Alonzo's cheek and said, "I haven't felt this way about anyone since I met Jarrod. I think we'd all be good together. I know a lot of three-way relationships that work out very well."

They all started laughing and Jarrod pulled out. He grabbed Alonzo and turned him over, and entered him again while he was on his back. Jarrod was one of those guys who didn't go soft right away. When Jarrod entered Alonzo in this position, Kyle leaned over and started kissing Alonzo on the mouth. While they kissed, Alonzo spread his legs, reached down with his right hand, and felt the base of Jarrod's shaft between the lips of his anus. He wished he had a mirror to see what it looked like.

But the minute Kyle inserted his tongue, the hotel room door blasted open and someone with an unusual costume stomped into the room. Alonzo was still on his back, with his legs wide open and Jarrod's dick still up his ass. When he glanced up, he recognized the costume immediately. It resembled an old-fashioned Italian clown costume, but not exactly a clown costume. He'd seen costumes like this many times at street fairs and events. The majority of the costume consisted of a tight bodysuit in different shades of red, yellow, green, gold, and black in a harlequin pattern. It was so tight the outline of the man's penis was visible. There were puffy, white long sleeves, with thin black ribbons tied into bows at the wrist. The black leather boots had three-inch heels and pointy toes. The man wore a large, wide-brimmed hat tipped to the side, with a huge white plume on the right. It was a uniform that could have been mistaken for a court jester or fool. The last time Alonzo had seen anyone wear a costume like this he'd been in Italy, running for his life. He gulped and held his breath when he realized they'd found him in America.

Kyle's head went up. "Dude, what the fuck?" He reached down and covered his dick with both hands.

Jarrod pulled out of Alonzo and sat up straight. He gaped at the man in the costume and said, "Get the fuck out of here, asshole." He made no attempt to cover his dick.

The man in the costume had dark hair and a large Roman nose. He reached into his pocket, pulled out a revolver, and pointed it toward the bed. He spoke with a thick Italian accent. He shook the gun at Alonzo and said, "Where is it?" Then he glanced down at the way Alonzo's legs were spread and said, "Whore, faggot," with such disdain that for a moment Alonzo thought he might spit on the floor.

When the clown started to shake the gun, Kyle jumped out of bed and ran for his clothes. Jarrod wasn't far behind. He grabbed his dick, climbed out of bed, and ran to the pile of clothes Kyle was rummaging through. Kyle looked at Jarrod and said, "I told you there was something too good about him. But you never trust my instincts."

"Shut the fuck up and let's get the fuck out of here, dude," Jarrod said. "Seriously, man. I'm like ready to fucking shit myself. This is worse than that time we got arrested for fucking that ginger dude in the school bus behind the bowling alley in Bakersfield."

Kyle flung him a glare. "That was all your fault, too, asswipe. I didn't want to do it. I told you Bakersfield could be trouble. The bus was too open and I knew anyone could see us. But no, you wouldn't listen. You needed to fuck ginger ass that night."

"You wanted to tap that ginger dude just as bad as I did."

While Kyle and Jarrod bickered, the man pointed the gun at Alonzo and said, "Tell me where it is, *faggot*, whore." He laughed. "And then maybe I'll fuck you myself tonight, pussy boy. I'll bet you'd like me to do that to you. I got a nice big sausage right here." He reached down and grabbed his crotch.

Alonzo went up on his knees and squared his back. He lifted his chin and glared at the man with the gun. Then he set his jaw and lifted his right hand. He made a fist and extended his index finger and pinky finger and leaned forward. While he jerked his arm backward and forward he said,

"You are the worst of all that is evil and the master of all that is sinful. I command the powers of all that is good and kind to fill me with love, and I cast the evil eye upon your wretched soul and put an end to it."

As Alonzo lifted his arm higher, the two jocks stopped and glanced at what he was doing. They were almost dressed now. Their pants were up and their shirts were on. They held their shoes against their stomachs and their mouths were open.

The man stepped back and said, "*faggot.*" But there was a look of sheer terror on his face as he glanced at the way Alonzo was gesturing to him. Beads of perspiration started to stream from his temples and he began to sway from one side to the other. He turned an unusual shade of red and his chest began to heave.

Alonzo continued to gesture, with his index finger and pinky finger, moving his arm backward and forward. "Die, you decrepit devil. I spit on your grave. Fall down right here in this room and drop dead. Go straight to the devil where you belong."

The two jocks exchanged a quick glance.

The clown grabbed his chest and dropped the gun. He stumbled backward into a Danish modern chair covered in orange vinyl and his face turned from red to a blue-gray. Then he clutched his chest with his other hand and gasped for air. A second later, he fell to the floor in a state of unconsciousness.

When Alonzo saw what he'd done, he lowered his arm and unclenched his fist. He climbed off the bed and stood naked over the man in the unusual costume. Up close, he was older than Alonzo had first thought he was. From the wrinkles around his eyes and lips, Alonzo figured he was about 50 years old. Alonzo knew he would have to remove the costume now and dispose of it.

Kyle and Jarrod put on their shoes and Jarrod crossed over to where the man was sprawled out on the floor. He reached down to touch the man's pulse and looked up at Alonzo. "I think he's dead, dude. What the fuck just happened here?" He sent Kyle a backward glance and shrugged.

Kyle said, "I think we should call for help. I think he had a heart attack."

Alonzo ignored them. He knew what had happened and he knew who this man in the odd costume was. He looked up at the cracked hotel room ceiling and said, "I promised I'd do what I had to do and this was part of it. There was nothing else left to do. In the name of *Uomini Di*

Magia." His eyes glazed over and his voice became a stage whisper, speaking as if he were in a deep trance. He'd been taught how to use the powers of the evil eye at midnight on Christmas Eve many years ago by his grandmother. He'd never had to use it until now.

Jarrod blinked.

Kyle said, "Dude, this is really starting to freak me out."

Alonzo continued to ignore them, staring up at the ceiling. As nice as Kyle and Jarrod were, he was in America for one reason and he couldn't let two good-looking men get in his way.

That's when Jarrod grabbed Kyle's arm and said, "Let's go, man. This shit's too fucked up for me. I'm not into this weird shit. I'm like all shaky and sick to my stomach now." Then he yanked Kyle over the dead man in the costume, pulled him out of the room, and didn't look back once.

About the Author

Ryan Field is the author of over 100 published works of LGBT fiction, the best-selling Virgin Billionaire series, a PG-rated hetero romance that was featured on The Home Shopping Network titled, "Loving Daylight," and a few more works of full-length fiction with a pen name. He has worked in publishing for 20 years as a writer, editor, and associate editor. His work has been in Lambda Award winning anthologies and he's self-published a few novels with Ryan Field Press.

Other Riverdale Avenue Books Titles
By Ryan Field You Might Enjoy

The Wizard of Pride

A Starr is Born

Sleepless in San Francisco

Pretty Man

A Christmas Carl

Fangsters: Clan of the Jersey Boys
boys

Fangsters 2: Gangbang Fangsters

Valley of the Dudes

Stepbrothers in the Attic

Dancing Dirty

Other Titles by Ryan Field

Ryan Field Press Titles
A Life Filled with Awesome Love
A Regular Bud
A Sign from Heaven Above
A Young Widows Promise
All About Yves
Altered Parts
American Star
American Star II
An Officer and His Gentleman
Another Regular Bud
Baby Cakes
Big Bad And On Top
Billabong Bang
Bury it Officer
Cage James
Capping the Season
Captain Velvet's Velvet Box
Cherry Soda Cowboy
Cowboy Christmas Miracle
Cowboy Howdy
Cowboy Mike and Buddy Boy
Dirty Little Virgin
Field of Dreams
Four Feet Under
Four Gay Weddings and a Funeral
Gay Pride and Prejudice
He's Bewitched
Hot Italian Lover
Imperfect
In Their Prime
Internal Desires
It's Nice to be Naughty
Jolly Roger
Jonah Sweet of Delancey Street
Kendle's Fire

Kevin Loves Cowboys
Meadows Are Not Forever
Missing Jackson's Hole
My Fair Laddie
New Adult Love Story
Pumpkin Ravioli Boy
Ricky's Business
Rough Naked and in Love
Said With Care
Shakespeare's Lover
Sir, Yes Sir!
Skater Boy
Something for Saint Jude
Strawberries and Cream at the Plaza
Take Me Always
That Cowboy in the Window
The Arrangement
The Bachelor
The Buckhampton Country Club
The Computer Tutor Box
The Ghost and Mr. Moore
The Mile High Club
The Preacher's Husband
The Sheriff And The Outlaw
The Way We Almost Were
The Women Who Love To Love Gay Romance
Too Hard To Handle
Unabated
Uncertainty
Unmentionable: The Men Who Loved on the Titanic
Vance's Flame
Whatever Dude
When A Man Loves A Man
With this Cowboy I Love so Freely
You Missed a Spot Big Guy
Young Doughy Joey
Young Hung and Hitched

Bad Boy Billionaire Series
Cowboy in Love
Palm Beach Sex Scandal
Silicon Valley Sex Scandal
Small Town Romance Writer
The Actor Learning to Love
The Arrangement
The Ivy League Rake
The Vegas Shark
The Wall Street Shark

Chase Series
Chase of a Christmas Dream
Chase of a Dream - Abridged
Chase of a Dream - Unabridged
Chase of a Holy Ghost
Chase of a Lifetime
Chase of an Adventure: Fifty Shades of Gay

Down The Basement Series:
Down the Basement
Down the Basement II: Santa Saturday

Second Chance Series
Second Chance
Second Chance: His Only Choice
Second Chance: The Littlest Christmas Tree
Second Chance: The Sweetest Apple

The Virgin Billionaire Series
The Virgin Billionaire
The Virgin Billionaire and the Evil Twin
The Virgin Billionaire: Revenge
The Virgin Billionaire's Dream House
The Virgin Billionaire's Hot Amish Escapade
The Virgin Billionaire's Little Angel
The Virgin Billionaire's Reversal of Fortune
The Virgin Billionaire's Secret Baby
The Virgin Billionaire's Sexcellent Adventure
The Virgin Billionaire's Wedding

We hope that you enjoyed book one of *The Rainbow Detective* series! Please, consider leaving a review on either Amazon or Goodreads. Reviews are the life's blood of the independent author and publisher and would be greatly appreciated.

Want to keep up with the latest from Ryan Field and Riverdale Avenue Books? Sign up to our newsletter where you can find free books, exclusive promo codes and latest news:
https://preview.mailerlite.io/preview/1098983/sites/136486432257607665/0kJ9TD

Looking to be an ARC reader/reviewer? You can sign up to our Reviewer/ ARC Program at the link provided here:
https://preview.mailerlite.io/preview/1098983/sites/160569605411046909/pvCkb9?fresh=1